MASQUERADING WITH THE CEO

A WHAT HAPPENS IN **VEGAS** STORY

DAWN CHARTIER

Entangled Publishing, LLC
2614 South Timberline Road
Suite 109
Fort Collins, CO 80525
Visit our website at www.entangledpublishing.com.

Lovestruck is an imprint of Entangled Publishing, LLC.

Edited by Suzanne Evans
Cover design by Heather Howland
Cover art from 123RF.com

Manufactured in the United States of America

First Edition July 2015

I dedicate this novel to my family, friends and readers. I hope you enjoy this Vegas story as much as I enjoyed writing it.

Chapter One

With her three best friends by her side, Kylie Edwards sat in the back of the white stretch limo, excited that her life was about to change forever.

Her fingers brushed against her ivory silk wedding gown, designed especially for her by *the* Vera Wang. Compliments of her fiancé.

The gown was striking and sophisticated, yet simple in design—a description she'd always thought fit her. Striking and sophisticated also described the wealthy CEO of Trident Industries, her soon-to-be husband, Brett McAllister. But he was far from simple. He was so much more. She couldn't believe it. In only a few moments, she would be Mrs. McAllister.

It still felt like a dream. Millionaire playboy Brett McAllister had fallen in love with her. She had no idea why—but he had. The old saying "opposites attract" couldn't be any closer to the truth. The only flair she had was for interior design, thanks to an eye for color and details she'd inherited from her dad. Otherwise, there was really nothing special about her. Not until Brett. He made her *feel* special. Especially today.

She lifted a colorful pink, purple, and white bouquet of carnations and sniffed. The scent immediately made her think of her mother, who had died two years ago. *Your favorite, Mom.* A faint pang of heartache rose as it did often when she thought of her mom, but it was especially painful today. Kylie had refused to carry any other flower in her hands on this magical day. Everything was perfect, with the exception of her mother not being here to witness her only daughter getting married.

She sighed and shot a glance at Jan, who hadn't said much all day. Her best friend and maid of honor stared out of the tinted window, fidgeting with the ends of her lilac satin sash.

"You feelin' okay?"

Jan nodded but still didn't look in her direction.

Puzzled, Kylie faced Sara and Ashlyn on her other side, and they shrugged in unison.

She swiveled back toward Jan. "I'm the one who should be nervous. What's with you today?" Now that she thought about it, her friend had been acting a little strange for the last few weeks.

Jan shook her head. "Nothing."

Even though the absence of Kylie's mother was the most powerful thing in the car right now, Kylie wouldn't let it drop. "It's obviously something. Fess up."

Jan's gaze dipped to where her fingers fidgeted in her lap. "There is something I think you need to know before you marry Brett."

Kylie's glare shot to Jan's downturned face, trying to look her in the eye as a slice of fear cut across her chest. "What?"

"I hoped he would tell you, but—"

"Tell me what?" Her temple throbbed, and she stilled.

Jan raised her chin. Her mouth opened, closed, then opened again. "I slept with Brett."

Kylie flinched. Pain splintered deep into her temple, and her stomach twisted. With four simple words, her world stopped, tilted, and turned upside down.

Jan's eyes filled. "I'm so sorry. I begged Brett to confess weeks ago. I'm only saying something now because I'm your friend. I don't want you to marry that snake."

"You're her *friend*?" Ashlyn coughed. "Right."

"Back-stabbing bitch," Sara snapped.

The bickering began, but their voices sounded distant. Kylie slid deep into her inner hiding place. *No.* She had to have misunderstood. Brett wouldn't do that. But why would Jan lie? Did Jan want Brett for herself?

"Look. I didn't have to tell her, but that man doesn't deserve either of us." Jan wrapped her arms around her waist, pretending to be the victim.

How dare Jan act innocent when she was clearly the villain? Kylie could easily open the car door and push Jan out.

But more so, Kylie wanted out of the limo. She wanted to run. She wanted to die.

She squeezed her eyes shut. *How could they betray me?* She tried to inhale through burning lungs. *I was so sure he loved me.*

I can't breathe. I can't breathe. God help me.

She stared at her mother's favorite flowers, now lying by her feet in a taunting, multi-colored pile. "Pull over," she said. The carnation scent was now sickeningly sweet.

The limo continued rolling.

"Pull. Over." The driver finally noticed her in the rearview mirror, and she mouthed again, "Pull over."

He squinted as though he hadn't read her lips correctly, but she nodded, confirming the words.

It seemed like an eternity before they stopped. She stared out the front windshield and almost pitched her breakfast when she saw the chapel only a hundred or so feet away. Friends and family entered the church, and judging by the long line of parked cars, more were inside, waiting on her arrival. Waiting to share this special moment of her life with her. *How can I face them? How can I face my dad? How can I disappoint him again? He'll never let me live this one down. Ever.*

She swallowed hard, and her heart shriveled like a dried prune.

Now it was *she* who couldn't look at Jan—not without losing the yogurt and cup of fruit she'd forced down hours ago.

A lump of fear mixed with hatred clawed its way up her throat.

"Get out." Her voice sounded hard and raw. Devastated.

"I'm sorry, Ky." Jan picked at her sleeve, her face a pale shade of green. "Brett wouldn't leave me alone. I tried to stay away, but you know how persuasive he is when he wants something."

Kylie's insides ignited, and if she could have shot fire out of her eyes, she would have. Instead, she glared straight ahead. "I. Said. Get. Out."

. . .

"Get out of bed, Ky," a voice called out.

Kylie lifted her head slightly off the pillow. Damn it. She'd finally fallen asleep a half an hour ago. What day was it? Had it already been a week since her wedding day? No matter. She still wasn't ready to talk to anyone. Whoever it was could wait, especially Brett, but the voice was too soft to be Brett's.

Ring. Ring. Ring. Kylie lifted the receiver to her mouth. "Go away," she said into the phone and placed it on the nightstand. She only wanted sleep. No. Not true. She wanted to die.

She raised her head again. Hell. It wasn't the phone ringing, but someone ringing the buzzer on the door. *Yep, that's what happens when you only sleep a few hours each night.* The incessant ringing and pounding yanked her from her sleepy state. Reaching for the lamp in the dark, she knocked Ashlyn's manuscript off the nightstand. "Dammit."

Bang. Bang. Bang.

"We know you're in there, Ky," Ashlyn's voice came from the other side of her front door.

Ash needed to get a clue.

Bang. Bang. Bang.

Fine. Kylie slid out of bed and walked down the hall, her too-long sweatpants dragging along the carpet. She yanked the door open and glared at her friends.

"Go away. I'm fine." She started to close the door, but Sara's foot slid into the doorway, stopping it from closing.

Sara and Ash glared at her. "The hell you are," Ash said.

I look that bad? Probably worse than bad. Before she could force the door shut, they pushed past her to the table with a bag and three cups of what smelled like coffee.

"I bet you haven't eaten in days." Sara dropped the bag on the table and reached in, pulling out a bagel. "You love breakfast, so sit. Eat."

Kylie glared at the bagel. She couldn't touch food. The coffee smelled like her favorite mocha-mint, though, and she sort of wanted it. "I can't."

"We aren't leaving until you eat something. This isn't you, Ky. You have to get out of this slump. At least get out of those pj's and bathe!" Sara leaned over the table and pushed a coffee cup toward her. "I miss my sappy-go-lucky friend."

"Sappy?" She dipped her head to her arm and sniffed. She had bathed, maybe…okay, twice since that day. Hygiene wasn't her utmost priority right now anyway. She couldn't see much through the anger and hurt.

Ash patted her hand. "Exactly. Don't let that bitch and the CEO dick-wad ruin your life."

"Too late. My life is ruined." She sank into the chair and took a grudging sip of her latte.

"You still have lots to be thankful for. One, you didn't marry that asshole. Two, you have a great job at your dad's design firm. Three, you have this freakin' awesome condo in the heart of Phoenix." Ash turned in a circle. "Look around you."

All of it was true. But what did it matter if she had no one to share it with? She knew she was wallowing, but damn it, she deserved a pity party right now. "Y'all don't get it. I thought he was truly the one. Instead, he betrayed me with one of my closest friends."

"You still got us," Sara said, "and that's why we're here."

"You know what I mean. I want someone to wake up with every morning. I want someone to *truly* love me." This was what she'd always dreamed of. Now what did she have left to dream about? God, she was pitiful. Still. She didn't want to end up like her father. All he cared about was money and power. Well, look where that got him. Look where it got Brett. Asshole.

For a short while, soon after her mother died, her father had been so distraught. No amount of money could stop her mother's cancer. So Kylie invited him over a few times to visit with her. She tried to break the ice between them, but he never had anything good to say, and most of the time he was half-drunk. He found a quick replacement for her mother, and he didn't care if the woman loved him or not. He could control her, and she used him. The sad part was that neither of them cared. He spoiled his fiancée and blew money on more plastic surgeries than anyone could possibly need, but in return, she kept him company in bed. A loveless marriage eats at the soul. *I won't be like him.*

Brett had just proved that all CEOs must be emotionless like her father.

But she couldn't go through this pain again. The ache ate a hole in her heart. "I'm pathetic," she said and dropped her head in her hands.

"Exactly. And we are here to fix that." Sara cast a sly smile in Ash's direction. "Tell her."

Chapter Two

Jake Royale sat behind his desk at his hotel and casino, Masquerade, reviewing the financials with his advisor. A headache grew by the second. "This doesn't look good, Pat."

"Jake, it's not bad." Patrick crossed his legs and eased back in the chair across from him. "It's to be expected when a new casino opens next door. It will pick up again. Plus, we are booked solid this weekend for that conference."

His jaw ached. "Expected or not, I don't like it." He shoved the reports across the desk. "When do our renovations begin?"

"I knew you'd ask, so I checked with Tad. You'll be glad to know the new design firm called half an hour ago and wants to meet this weekend."

"Good. I'm ready to do whatever it takes." Jake never liked coming in second, and with the brand new casino next door, Masquerade needed refreshing. He'd already approved the budget.

Though he worried about the competition, there was something else nagging him. Something that had been nagging him for a long time. Like a part of his life was missing. He pushed the thought to the side.

Jake leaned back in his leather chair after Pat left and glanced at the monitors on the wall. He watched the live feed from the front entrance. "Is that…?" He squinted, then leapt from his chair. His seat flung backward and bumped into the credenza. "Fuck. Me. He's back."

• • •

"You don't have a say in this." A slow smile eased across Ashlyn's lips. "We're taking you to Vegas, baby."

"No. No. No. I'm not going to the biggest elopement city in the world."

Less than six hours after she'd said those words, Kylie grabbed her luggage off of the carousel at the Vegas airport. Her friends hadn't given her a choice. They'd packed her clothing, and she'd thrown in her design charts and samples after her "so-called" friends called her dad and begged him to give Kylie the casino job. They'd known it was the only way she'd agree to go. Shockingly, their plan worked.

So here she stood at the airport in Vegas. At least she had her work and her father's reluctant blessing to try impressing their new client with her designs. He'd already been planning to meet this casino client later this week, but allowed her to go in his place—something that had never happened in her entire life. She wasn't sure why he'd never given her a chance to prove herself before with big clients. Other than a few tiny flooring screw ups, she'd been a pretty good employee overall. She'd show him this time. She'd make him proud.

Ash was there for a romance writers' conference, but Kylie had a job to do.

She couldn't miss this chance to prove she could handle a job by herself. He'd made her work harder and longer than any of his other employees, always saying he couldn't let anyone think she was getting special treatment from the boss. Hell, the last four years she'd gotten just the opposite. Maybe he'd give her the promotion to senior designer after this. *In your dreams.* Dreams were all she had now. Kylie lowered her sunglasses from the top of her head, but she still had to shield her eyes as they walked out of the airport. The dry heat sucked all the air from her lungs and the moisture from her skin within seconds.

"What happens in Vegas..." Ash said.

"Stays in Vegas," Sara finished.

Kylie nodded, faking interest. While Ash and Sara were here to party with a bunch of authors, readers and cover models, she would, instead, bury herself in work so she wouldn't think about—

A horn blew, and she jerked around. Her eyes widened and her hands clamped over her mouth as she stared ahead at the white limo rolling to a stop directly in front of her. *The same kind of limo I used for my wedding.* Her breath came out in short bursts, and memories of that horrifying day began to suffocate her. Of how the limo driver had dropped her off at home while Sara and Ashlyn informed everyone at the church, including her dad, that she wasn't coming. "Um. Ash? Sara?"

Sara spotted the limo and then glanced at her. Sara must

have understood that seeing the white limo made her think of the moment when she discovered how life could change in a split second. "Shit." She searched the pickup area. "It's okay. We won't take a limo. Look." Sara pointed. "There's a shuttle bus for the hotel pulling away. Run."

Kylie barely noticed the Cinderella carriage spectacle rising out of the fountain in front of Masquerade Hotel and Casino before she hurried inside. The sweat that formed on her back dried before it had time to soak her shirt. She removed her large sunglasses, instantly eyeing the massive poles with ribbons and beads flanking the registration area, and then the huge jester hat that occupied the center of the lobby caught her eye.

Somehow the Bourbon Street decor didn't appear as gaudy as her father had warned or the pictures had shown, but it still needed some serious updating, and she was just the girl to do it. The new plan was to bury herself in this project for the next six months—that is, if the owner liked her designs. *He will. He has to.*

Screams of laughter filled the area as several women entered the lobby. Kylie inwardly cringed. *Yep. Romance Lovers Convention.* Why she'd let Ashlyn talk her into coming, she'd never know. She didn't actually have a choice, now that she thought about it. *They did you a favor, admit it. Daddy never listened to your pleas when you'd asked for a project on your own, so now you have an opportunity to prove yourself because of them.*

Ashlyn's hand shot out and gripped her wrist. She

squealed like a teenager.

Kylie's heart jumped. "What's wrong?"

Ash covered her mouth, and her voice sounded muffled. "Do you know who that is?"

Sara and Kylie both rolled their eyes. *Here we go.*

"That's freakin' J.R. Ohmygod!" Ash jumped up and down.

Kylie spotted the thin blonde wearing dark sunglasses. That had to be J.R. surrounded by fans. "Go get her autograph."

"Not here. Maybe tomorrow at the literary signing, and if not there, I'll stalk her at the Grand Masquerade ball…or maybe she'll be at the publisher's party."

"I'm going to check in," Sara said, not fazed. Sara didn't read much, unless it was a murder mystery or law books. It was the male model-watching and parties that convinced Sara to attend with Ash each year.

Kylie enjoyed almost all romance novels, but she didn't recognize too many authors by their faces, not like Ash did, although the woman with dark hair and blue highlights getting into an elevator did look a lot like Gina Maxwell. *Dang it.* She hadn't had time to pack her Cinderella series books so she could grab her autograph.

After checking in, a man who sort of resembled a young Leonard Nimoy helped them with their luggage. Ash had given up her room for Kylie, knowing she'd want the room to herself. "We'll only be next door, Ky."

"You with the writers' convention?" the concierge asked.

"No, not really," Kylie answered, eyeing the man's name tag that read Will. "I'm just along for the ride. My friend, Ash is an author though. I'm here for a meeting with Mr. Royale and his design team." *And to try and forget about a wedding that never happened and a bitch of an ex-best friend.*

"Then I'd better be on my best behavior," Will said. "Let me know if I can get you and your friends anything." He handed her his card. "I only give this to our special guests. Call if you need anything at all."

How sweet of him. She was beginning to think that men with regular jobs were much more friendly and real than typical stuffed-suit men. "Thanks." She slipped him a twenty before he left.

Kylie observed the room and cataloged the decor from floor to ceiling. The suite wasn't bad either, but it would be better once she was done with it. Internally, she was picturing the sage family color charts she'd chosen, though the golden palettes were pretty too.

Proud of her designs, she couldn't wait to showcase her boards and finish samples. Mr. Williams from The Vault Casino next door would regret not choosing her design over Jerk B's design. Jerk B was better known in her father's company as Billy, her father's right-hand man.

A tightening in her stomach eased some as a heavy sigh escaped. One day…

She examined the bathroom. *Spacious. Sleek.* Masquerade had more charm than The Vault—it just needed a little TLC. Like her.

Sara swung open the adjoining door. "You're not work-ing, are you? We have to be ready in thirty minutes."

"I'm unpacking, and then I need to finish reading Ash-lyn's manuscript. Y'all go without me." Kylie unzipped her suitcase.

"Uh. No you're not." Ash strolled in the room. "My book isn't due yet, and we have big plans for you."

• • •

Jake rushed out of his private elevator, meeting with his chief of surveillance and best friend, Macon Spelling, in the middle of the casino. "You saw him?"

Macon nodded and folded his arms. "I got it. Go back to whatever you were doing. Let me do my job."

Macon knew better. Jake would never let it go. Not this time. The urge to pound his fist through something grew strong. The muscles in his neck tightened.

The bastard next door had already stolen several of Jake's employees, promising them things that the asshole would never deliver.

As Jake made his way down the long corridor with Macon by his side, they passed the Barakoa coffee bar, a server dropped a tray full of frappes and lattes in front of him.

Her eyes widened when she noticed he was watching and realized who he was. "Excuse me, sir."

Most CEOs weren't hands on, but Jake made a promise to himself that he would get to know as many employees as possible. Not to mention he was a control freak, or so he was told. He motioned for Macon to assist her, but then he saw. The server's stomach protruded, as though she were ready to have a baby…right now. He grabbed Macon's arm to stop him.

"I'm so sorry, Mr. Royale." The young lady awkwardly bent down, laboring to pick up the mess.

He leaned over, cupped her elbow and helped her up. "Macon, call housekeeping immediately."

Macon nodded and radioed it in.

The waitress shied away and her cheeks burned red. "Please. Don't fire me." She held her stomach.

She seemed to mistake his concern for anger. Why was she wearing such a short skirt and low-cut shirt? She shouldn't be dressed like this. Especially not right now.

"What's your name?" he asked. He clearly read Megan on her name tag, but he wanted her to relax so she wouldn't go into labor right this second.

She lowered her trembling chin. "Meg Monroe."

"Come." He walked her to an empty slot machine seat in a quiet area of the high roller's gambling area next to the Topenga Grill. "Sit, Meg." She sat. "What are you having?"

Meg blinked rapidly. "A girl. She's due in three weeks, sir."

Jake thought back to his mom bussing tables when she was pregnant with his younger sister while he stayed home alone. "How are your feet?"

"My—my feet?" she asked, frowning.

"Swelling, huh? I bet your back is aching too," he said matter-of-factly.

Her jaw dropped. "Yes, sir." She tilted her head as if wondering how he would know such a thing.

"I guessed." *Liar.* "Meg, you can't waitress here anymore."

She shook her head slightly, like she was in denial. "Why? I promise I won't be clumsy again." Tears filled her eyes. "Please, I need this job."

He should have explained first. "I'm not firing you. Just moving you to another department. *Where you can sit most of the day.* But today, right now—go home. Get off your feet."

Her eyes filled. "I can't. I need my pay."

"You will be compensated for today. Now go home."

The waitress wiped tears from her cheeks. "Thank you,

sir. Thank you. Thank you."

Jake walked away, not wanting or needing to hear her thanks. Instead, he mentally berated himself for not noticing her sooner. Next board meeting, he would be sure to ask HR to move any pregnant waitresses, if there were any, to other positions temporarily.

"Mighty nice of you," Macon said. "As usual."

Jake ignored him, but his adrenaline spiked. "Where is that thief bastard?"

"In the Karaoke Lounge." He turned and headed in that direction.

Macon and Jake had grown up together in the same trailer park, both dirt poor. "Asshole doesn't sell the good shit at his own bar so he needed to come here?" Jake was almost sprinting. *And steal your employees. Prick's never gotten over the past.*

Jake picked up his pace and quickly found Mark Williams, his wannabe rival, drinking a glass of his best scotch. He slid onto the barstool next to him and the bartender, Mike, immediately placed an on-the-rocks glass filled with what looked like bourbon in front of him. Except his drink wasn't what everyone thought. A special bourbon bottle sat in the back corner just for him. Plain old Coke. Not one drop of liquor.

After his drunken father had left him and his pregnant mother, he vowed to never touch the stuff. It had taken him ten years of heavily drinking to remember that promise, though.

Macon stood behind Mark, his arms folded across his broad chest.

"Enjoying our scotch?" Jake asked with ice in his tone.

"Jake." Mark nodded, raised his glass, and motioned to the bartender for another one. Mark glanced behind him. "Macon." He made another slight nod.

"What's wrong, Williams? The Vault's scotch is the cheap stuff?" Macon moved in closer.

"Call your guard dog off, Jake."

Macon's hands clenched. "Say the word, Boss. Say the word."

Jake ignored their requests. "Why are you here?"

"I'm looking for someone."

"Another employee of mine? Why not meet them in your own club?" Jake fisted his hands, barely holding control of his anger. Now wasn't the time — or the place.

"I'm not the one who steals things from others." Mark's jaw clearly tensed at the mention of his ex-girlfriend. If only she had stayed with Mark instead of moving into his Jake's life. His life would have been so much better. "Besides, I didn't say I was meeting someone. I said I was looking for someone. A lady friend." Mark chugged the rest of his drink down this throat, slammed the glass on the bar, then stood. "Looks like she isn't here."

Mark didn't deny pilfering from him, and Jake couldn't help but wonder if he was referring to his hostess, Patricia. She'd been acting a little strange lately. He glanced around realizing he hadn't seen her at all today.

Macon inched back, barely allowing the jerk to squeeze past. "Want me to follow, Boss?"

"No." Jake watched Williams disappear from the bar and get lost in a big group of loud women, and then he glanced at a banner sign near the lobby welcoming the Romance Lovers Convention attendees. Of course it was that time of year again where thousands of romance writers and readers were due in this week. "Leave him. We have other concerns right now."

"Don't worry. Patricia has everything under control," Macon said.

Maybe, but Patricia seemed to keep disappearing whenever he was around. He wasn't sure, but he got the feeling she was hiding something. *Maybe Mark got to her too.* "I'm sure she does, but keep an eye on her anyway."

Techno music suddenly blared from the speakers.

Macon turned and stared at the cute, brown-eyed DJ while she set up her equipment. "You ready for tonight, Pasha?" he asked.

Jake silently groaned. It was hard keeping his eyes off of the beauty, even though she wasn't his type. They had needed a DJ desperately, and she'd proven to be one of the best.

Pasha nodded. "Always ready," she said in her sweet Turkish accent. "You coming to watch, yes?"

"If the boss man lets me," Macon said.

Jake folded his arms. Macon didn't need his approval, but he pretended to in front of other employees. "Let Pasha do her job and you do yours," he ordered, and they walked out of the Karaoke Lounge.

Three giggling women cut in front of them.

"Saweet," Macon said, barely loud enough for Jake's ears.

"Keep your pants on. They're writers, not strippers."

"You forget what happened last year?" Macon asked. "Besides, I like the literary type—the erotic literary that is."

Jake shook his head. He hadn't forgotten. Several of the

authors got word of who he was and tried seducing him, insisting he could be a cover model for their books. And there was one particular publisher he'd never forget. She'd practically bribed him with her *ass*ets. "On your own time."

"You're blind. The hot babe in blue is giving you the sweet eye."

Jake turned in the opposite direction. "I'm married already—to the casino."

"Yeah. Don't I know, bro."

"Someone has to keep this place running while others are chasing women or letting women chase them."

"Ouch." Macon's gaze shot back to the woman in the blue skirt. "You're just chicken someone will run off with all your money, and you'll be poor again."

"No. I don't like being used is all," Jake said. Macon joked, but it still stung. "Don't you have a job to do?" His ex had been nothing but a gold digger, but it hadn't said much about his own character for being so damn blind. No one would ever use him like that ever again.

"Always."

"Then go tell Perry and Will to be on the lookout for that bastard Mark, and if he steps foot in my casino again have them call me ASAP. I don't care what time, day or night."

Jake marched by the blackjack tables, poker tables, and the gift shop, and then recalled he was almost out of his favorite orange Tic Tacs. Macon was slipping with the one nice gesture he had consistently made over the years. Tic Tac delivery. Jake hurried into the gift shop, grabbing several packs, shoving some in his pants pockets. As he twisted around, he ran smack into a woman.

The brunette glared at him, annoyed.

"Watch where you're going, buddy." Her lips thinned.

Buddy?

He continued to stare, even though it was rude. She was kind of cute. Her cheeks turned rosy, and the red tint traveled down the V of her shirt. He realized a little too late that he was checking out her full breasts when she covered herself with a bag of fluffy Cheetos and huffed.

Cat had his tongue while he gawked at her like an idiot. "Sor—"

"Geesh. Thanks for the help, jackass." She knelt and picked up other junk food items from the floor and then stormed off.

Jackass. Jake remembered to breathe and eased out of the shop, feeling as if he'd been hit with a thousand pounds of gambling chips. Someone had pissed her off bad, unless she was always like that. *Women.*

. . .

Stunned, Kylie hid on the next aisle. The guy wasn't just rude, staring where he shouldn't be, he was also a thief.

But that wasn't what had upset her. The moment she'd seen him walk through the door, she'd noticed the way he carried himself—like one of those executive jerk types. Just like her ex. Just like her emotionless father. That had to be why she'd turned on the bitch-switch so easily. It surely wasn't because of those gorgeous bedroom-green eyes. The rare sexy color you see on a handful of movie stars. *No, that couldn't be it.*

Her anger grew, heating her face and neck. *You're pissed because you're attracted to him. A thief. Geesh. That's a new low.*

"Sara. Hey, did you see that?" Surprised as hell by her attraction to the sex-on-a-stick man, Kylie peeked around the corner and watched the thief with the Hollywood-intense eyes. The sharp gray suit strolled right out of the shop like he owned the place. *The nerve of some people.*

He stood tall, and his midnight hair curled lightly on the ends, and yet was neatly trimmed. From the back, he resembled a certain CEO asshole. But CEOs didn't steal breath mints. Did they?

"See what?" Sara asked.

"That guy. He just hijacked some Tic Tacs, and walked right outta here without paying. Mints, of all things." She huffed, still upset at herself for not knowing *why* she was so upset.

"Mints?" Sara dropped her sunblock and gum on the checkout counter and leaned back. "Who, him? The hot James Bond look-alike who just glanced over his shoulder?"

Kylie scooted behind Sara, her throat suddenly dry. "Yeah. Him. Though I wouldn't call a thief a hottie." Except she would be lying if she admitted he wasn't a spitting image of the latest Bond—with darker hair and prettier eyes— but hottie or not, the man stole. When it was Kylie's turn to check out, she decided to tell the cashier. "Ma'am. That man," she gestured, "stole some items. I think you should call security."

"Not again." The cashier grabbed her phone, then leaned over her counter. "Tic Tacs? Oh. That's Macon, and he *is* security." She put the receiver down. "He's stealing for Mr. Royale, the owner." The cashier squinted and pulled out eyeglasses from beneath the register. "I'm blind as a bat for seeing distance without these glasses. Maybe? Wait. Is that…?"

The two men walked out of sight. "Hmm. I'm not sure. I think that was him." The clerk shrugged. "If he took orange Tic Tacs, then it had to be."

Jake Royale is a Tic Tac junkie. Who knew? Kylie couldn't wait to officially meet the owner this weekend. Maybe she'd bring him his favorite breath mints to break the ice. "Well, I hope so. I hate thieves." *And liars. And cheaters. And power-hungry CEOs.* She paid for her iced mocha-mint coffee, chips, and cookies and then left the gift shop, gulping the coffee to satisfy her sudden thirst.

Loads of women strolled around half in a daze, maybe lost, with stuffed conference tote bags, but the sexy man called Macon was gone.

Ashlyn caught up with them out in the corridor. "Look what I found in the souvenir shop. It's perfect for you." She fished in the bag and pulled out a beautiful feathered and sequined mask. The fire red and black colors were gorgeous, but no way.

"I'm not wearing that," Kylie's voice raised over the gaming machines' clatter.

"You are," she corrected, waving the mask. "At my publisher's costume party. You can do whatever you want, and no one will be the wiser."

"I'll know, and I won't be wiser." She turned around. Her breath caught, and she became aware of her own heartbeat racing out of control. There he was. Macon, the security dude, was talking to the pit boss and another guy near the roulette table, and as if he knew she was watching him, he glanced in her direction. Liquid pooled in her mouth, and she swallowed. *Why on earth are you so attracted to him? Stop. Just stop.* The other big man standing next to him turned as well. The temperature rose ten degrees in her cheeks and some places she'd rather ignore right now. *Crap.* She faced Ashlyn, not too happy she'd let him see her blush like a teenager.

She blamed it on not having sex for the last six months. Her ex-fiancé said it would make their wedding night more special. *Asshole.* She wrung her hands together. She should have known then that he was cheating, but she'd buried her head in planning a ridiculous wedding. Believing in a stupid ceremony fairytale was her fault, but damn Brett for making her abstain. Now she was horny, not to mention a bit lonely.

Ashlyn placed the sensual mask in her hand. "Have fun, Ky."

A brief vision of running her hands over the security guy's naked chest flashed through her mind. *Um. No. You can't. Don't be stupid.* She couldn't believe she was even thinking of approaching a guy after what she'd been through. She couldn't imagine putting her heart on the line again. But if no one knew it was her…and she kept her heart to herself…

No strings. Just sex. Maybe…

Chapter Three

A few hours later, Kylie and Sara lounged by the pool while Ashlyn attended a few writers' workshops. After the classes, they would eat and get ready for Ashlyn's publisher's masquerade party. It wouldn't take her long to get ready. Hiding your identity had its advantages. Who'd know what she looked like beneath? Maybe her friends were right—it was time to let loose and have some fun.

She swirled the straw in her frozen Banana Orgasm, and her thoughts turned back to the sexy security guy, Macon. *Forget him. And you would be on the rebound. But wouldn't sex with no strings be the perfect rebound? Maybe.*

But that was the point wasn't it? This guy wasn't a CEO like her ex. *Or like Dad.* Men who only cared about one thing—making it to the top and screwing everyone over in the process to reach it. Macon was regular. Not in looks, *God, so not in looks.* But in profession, yes. Security professionals were supposed to be trustworthy people, weren't they? *No. No. No.*

The mask entered her mind again. No. It was a dumb thought. He probably wouldn't be there anyway. The man couldn't work 24/7. She pushed the stupid idea out of her head. She needed to figure out a way of not wearing it. *If you wore it you could at least look, but don't touch*, she thought to herself.

"What?" Sara raised her sunglasses. "Don't touch who?"

"Talking to myself is all." Crud, she hadn't realized she'd said that out loud.

Sara arched a brow. "Right. Spill it."

"Nothing." She snatched Ash's manuscript and a red pen from the side table to make it appear that what she had said was a slip that meant nothing. But damn it, she couldn't get the Tic Tac man out of her crazy head.

Sara jerked the pen from her. "I'll be the judge of that. Talk."

Ugh. Kylie huffed, lounged back, and watched several women wearing little-to-nothing bikinis goofing off in the pool. There weren't many men here, except for a handful of beefy, over-tanned, oily cover models, but she had no interest in them whatsoever. *Probably married or gay anyway.* At least that's what she wanted to believe. She observed the old blue one-piece she was wearing. *No man would look at you in this grandma suit.* Plus, most men liked their women to look like sticks. She noted her curvy hips, definitely far from pretzel-stick size. She scooted further down in her lounger and closed her eyes. *Like that will help.*

"Helloooo. Tell me before I do something to embarrass you." The lounger creaked as Sara shifted, probably now facing her.

She opened her eyes. "Fine. Remember at the gift shop—the security guy stealing Tic Tacs?"

"What did the cashier call him? Oh yeah, Macon. Mr. GQ. Bond. How could I forget?" Sara searched to the left and right. "That's who you have the hots for? Oh, girl, you need to find him and touch him…everywhere. Where is he anyway?"

"I don't want to touch him. I'm done with men, like I said before." Kylie took another sip of her frozen drink, and her brain manifested a slight buzz. *Slow down.* She closed her eyes, gaining her balance. *Inhale. Exhale.*

"Not all men, right? Not men like Macon. I saw the way your mouth dropped open when you stared at him."

The hairs on her arms rose, and the nagging feeling that she was being watched was strong. "Stop it."

"Stop what?" Sara asked.

"Looking at me. I told you. I don't want to touch any man ever again." *Liar.*

"I'm not looking at you. And you do want to touch him or you wouldn't have brought him up. You think he's hot. You think he's sexy," Sara sang. "Wait 'til I tell Ash. She'll have the two of you hooked up by the end of the night."

"Don't you dare." Drinking one stupid drink had given her a loose tongue. "If you tell Ash about the Tic Tac thief, I'll never talk to you again."

"He wasn't stealing, remember. But I'm still telling. Ash and I have made it our goal to get you out of prim-and-proper mode and get you laid. It's time you let loose and have some fun."

"Laid? Prim and proper, huh?" She squeezed her lids tight. Is that what everyone thought of her? A stick in the mud. A boring old maid. Maybe so, but that wasn't who she really was on the inside. Broken yes, but not boring and proper. *Or am I?*

Whatever. She'd had enough of men and humiliation to last a lifetime. *Don't go there. Don't go there.*

A shadow covered the delightful sunrays that had been warming her face, and she opened her eyes, ready to fuss at Sara once more. Instead, her flesh probably turned twenty-five shades of pink and red, like the variety colors on her designing boards and paint fans.

It wasn't Sara.

Chapter Four

He'd been standing behind the two women, including the one he'd nearly knocked over earlier. He hadn't meant to eavesdrop, but he couldn't stop listening. He'd searched for her for at least thirty minutes before he'd found her, wanting to apologize to her for being such an inconsiderate klutz, but then he heard her talking about Macon and the Tic Tacs he'd taken.

So, she thought he was someone else. He wasn't sure where she'd gotten that from, but then an idea hit him. A grin tugged at his lips. What if he let her believe he was Macon? No strings, casual conversation, and most importantly, no expectations.

There was no way in hell he'd let someone use him for his money again. And no fucking way he'd allow his heart to be ripped from his chest, stomped on, and shoved down his throat once more either. So here was his chance of seeing what she *really* thought about him.

See if the lady would like to have lunch with *him*, and not casino owner Jake Royale.

He wouldn't lie if she asked him, but assuming his identity incorrectly was her doing, not his. A knot tightened in his stomach.

"Do you mind? You are in my light." She frowned.

"Don't mind at all. Your face looks a little sunburned. Maybe you should sit in the shade." He didn't move. He couldn't. His nerve endings stirred while taking in her lovely curves.

Her mouth dropped open, and her cheeks grew darker.

Before she could reply he added, "I'd like to apologize for bumping into you earlier and not helping you pick up your snacks. I was in a hurry."

"I guess when the boss calls for his Tic Tacs, it's a state of an emergency."

Jake's brows plunged. It sure as hell was. He couldn't live without them. "Not exactly." He folded his arms, fighting the urge to pop one into his mouth right now. "However, it does matter that I apologize. I'm sorry."

The other woman cleared her throat. "We haven't met. I'm Sara and this is—"

"Ashlyn." The cute brunette cut her friend off like she'd just made the name up. Hadn't he overheard them talking about an Ashlyn? He could easily find out her name and would.

Sara made a funny face at the so-called Ashlyn. "We already know who you are, sweetie. You're Macon." Sara gave him a wide, toothy smile.

He shifted from foot to foot, then caught himself and stilled. "I'd like to make it up to you for being so rude to you earlier, Ashlyn. Let me buy you—and your friend—lunch or dinner."

Her skin paled, and out of the corner of his vision, he saw Sara nodding like a toy dog in back of a car window.

"That sounds like a good…" Sara began.

"We can't. We have a publisher's party to attend tonight, remember?" The sexy woman cut her friend off again.

Ouch. Rejected. Another first today. "Are you an author?"

Her eyes widened as though he'd called her bluff. "Er. Yes. Yes. I am." She chewed on her straw nervously.

"Interesting." He noticed the stack of papers sitting next to her. Maybe she was a writer. Maybe he misunderstood when he was eavesdropping by accident. "I wouldn't have pegged you as an author."

She blinked. "And why not? What does an author look like?"

"Well…" Tension built in his jaw. What he meant to say was she seemed rather on the reserved side compared to the other writers he'd run across today and those from last year's convention. Several wore red or black boas and Mardi Gras beads and carried on like married women at a bachelorette party. Free for the weekend to do what they pleased.

"That's what I thought," Ashlyn bit.

He nodded. This was not going like he'd imagined all afternoon. He'd pictured her agreeing to lunch and possibly dinner and dancing later. Instead, it was time to leave before he stuck his foot in his mouth again. He wasn't ready to give up on her just yet though, but for now he'd let her sunbathe in peace.

"Nice meeting you both." He faced Ashlyn. Her supple lips smirked as though bothered by his presence. "Maybe another time." Then he left, needing to talk to the real Macon.

• • •

Sara hit Kylie on the arm with her oversized, floppy white hat. "You liar. Why'd you pretend to be Ashlyn? That man is one fine specimen."

"Ouch. Stop that." Kylie leaned to the far side of the lounger. Maybe she shouldn't have pretended to be her friend, but she panicked. Too late now.

"Then why did you give a false name?" Sara fluffed her hat back out.

"I guess I freaked," she said. "See? I'm not ready." If only she was. Never in her life had a sexy man like him ever paid attention to her. Sure, Brett was handsome, but Macon was like sex on a stick with a side order of chocolate-covered strawberries. Her stomach growled.

Sara sighed. "I understand you're hurting, Ky. But once you realize you hit the jackpot by *not* marrying that scumbag, you'll eventually thank Jan. Let loose. Seriously. I promise it will help you get over Brett if you just let go of the past and have fun."

Kylie's pulse pounded in her ears. She snatched her towel and shoved Ash's manuscript into her beach bag. Maybe Sara was right. Maybe she should count her blessings and allow herself to have a little fun. What was the saying? *What happens in Vegas…shit.*

"I'll see you inside." As she walked past the pool, she noted a massive round, clear, Mardi Gras-style bead wall that showed inside the Karaoke Lounge. She spotted Macon inside chatting with a skinny, brown-haired beauty. Her body grew twitchy, and she sighed. Who the hell was she kidding? The man had only wanted to apologize to her anyway. He clearly wasn't interested in her womanly, curvy type, so she'd best keep moving along before he caught her dreaming of something she had no business dreaming about.

After showering, Kylie gawked in the mirror, still not believing what she saw. First she pretended she was Ash to Macon, and now she sported Ashlyn's tight, red dress.

Her buddies pushed into her bathroom.

"Ohmygod!" Ash squealed.

Sara wore a bright yellow number, and Ash had on a sky-blue, slinky dress.

"This is too short and too tight." Kylie pulled at the hem. What would her father say if he saw her now? He would not approve, that's for damn sure. What would her mother say if she were alive to see her? Ha. Mom would love it.

"It's perfect," Ash said, then poked her arm. "Hmm. I'm pissed it looks better on you though. You fill it way better than I do. In all the right places."

Kylie wiggled her butt. "Hips courtesy of Momma." A little sting pinched her heart. *I know, Mom. You'd tell me to get my ass out there, use those hips, and have fun. For you I'll at least get out of this room and try.*

The three of them quickly ate at the sushi bar, Masuku, and then strolled into the dark Club Pearl. It seemed the place to be. People filled the stages, dancing in costumes, several wearing barely anything. Wasn't this a publisher's party? Maybe it was open to the public. She bent over a little, observing how the dress had risen way too high. She tugged the hem down for the hundredth time. Feeling heavy inside and out, she thanked God for the mask.

A woman came in and spoke to Ashlyn, then quickly walked off to other people.

"The publisher's party has been moved to the Karaoke Lounge. Let's go."

Now was the perfect moment for an escape, but Sara quickly grabbed her arm and led her to the lounge. *Damn.*

It must not have been karaoke time yet, because a DJ pulsed alternative music from the back of the club near the stage, and the rhythm called to her, but she didn't dance ever—at least not in public. She observed the extravagant room. No upgrading would be necessary here or in Club Pearl.

With her feather mask on, her nerves weren't as bad. About eight bartenders manned the Mardi Gras bar. There were plenty of glass tables and wrought iron barstools scattered everywhere, and dancers perched on the rails above the bar, swinging around while men drooled below them. This was so not her, but it was too late to leave now. She'd give it thirty minutes, but then she was gone.

"It's crowded," she said.

Sara and Ash grabbed her arms and tugged her farther inside. They must've thought she was going to bolt. *I will, but not yet.*

Ashlyn introduced several of her writer friends, her agent, and a few bloggers and reviewers, and Kylie recognized a few names.

"Rebecca, I love your vampire series, and Robin, those romantic comedies, keep 'em coming." And was that the famous author Jade being dragged on stage with the half-naked dancers?

"Thanks. Ash told us about your horrible situation, and we're here to make sure you have a great time. So, let's go par-tay," Robin said.

Kylie shot Ash a frown. "Thanks for telling everyone."

"I love you, Ky. We just want you to have fun." Ash pulled her toward the dance floor.

Her heart leapt inside her throat. "Nooooooo," she said. "You know I don't dance."

"Here, drink this Roulette shot." Ash grabbed a shot from the waiter, thrust the glass in her hand, and waggled her eyebrows.

"A shot?" She eyed the exit. She should leave now. Instead, she downed the drink. "I need another." They dragged her toward the bar.

Sara and Ash each bought her one. "Down the hatch," they said.

"Down the hatch," Kylie repeated, then swallowed the liquor. It burned her throat like gasoline and stank like the strongest cold medicine she'd ever taken. "Yuck." She held her nose for the second shot. They weren't going to give up on her dancing. "I think I need one more before I get out there to shake my big ass."

"Back that ass up," Ash chanted with a fist pump. "One more, Mr. Bartender." Then she winked at him. "You know you could be one of the cover models here."

The bartender winked. "I've heard that a lot this week."

Kylie didn't recall stepping on the dance floor, yet there she was. A dozen or so people in the publishing industry danced around her. The DJ had stopped earlier, and now patrons sung to various party songs. Hell, she could sing better than them. *In your dreams.* And maybe she would. She had a nice buzz going. For the first time since that humiliating day, she was truly relaxed. Her hips swayed, and her arms swung high above her head. A slight grin spread without her forcing it to do so. And for the first time since she'd arrived, she was having a good time, and she didn't want the feeling to stop. This was exactly what she had needed.

The liquid courage made her a great dancer, and she let loose. Her arm caught on the mask; she'd forgotten she had the damn thing on. Reaching up to pull it off, she hesitated when she saw him. Her pulse hitched. *Damn.* Her entire body responded to him.

Bond. James Bond. She giggled. Macon was half-hidden in a private area off to the side near the sound equipment, his gaze glued to her. Her face heated. Did he know it was her?

He licked his bottom lip. Oh, God! He was hot. Hotter than all of these cover models put together. She raised her hair and fanned the back of her neck. Lord, his staring was making her burn between her thighs. Why weren't any women hanging off of him? Maybe it was that possessive glare he wore right now — aimed directly at her.

Dang. She spoke too soon. A beautiful, tall woman approached him. Her long blond curls fell forward as she bent over his table, whispering something in his ear. He shook his head. The Amazon kissed his cheek, then left.

Good. Keep walking, Barbie. Kylie continued dancing. A new person got on stage to sing a song, and the rhythm slowed, as did her swaying hips. His stare never left her. She liked it and did a subtle jig. Maybe she liked it a little too much.

What are you doing? Stop your drooling. Damn Roulette

shots. She finally turned, pretending to ignore him, yet her hips still swayed like a cat—no, more like a mountain lion—in heat, and a part of her, the much lower part, wished he would come to her. Make her purr. Make her rub his—shit. *Stop that.* She shook her head to clear out the liquid lust.

The song stopped, and the next thing she knew, Ash and Sara were dragging her up on stage. Before she could protest she was standing front and center at the microphone when the TV monitor showed the title, "Bad Romance."

She sent a glare at her friends on each side of her. They both laughed and then began to clap. Screw it. They wanted her to have fun, then by God, she would. The lyrics began on the screen, and she belted out the song in the loudest and most heartfelt voice she could. Sara was bent over laughing, along with some of the crowd, but the rest of the crowd was singing along. Some people covered their ears, though. Well, maybe she was too loud. She lowered her tune some, but right now she didn't care what anyone thought. "Bad Romance" was exactly the perfect song for her.

The song ended, and she bowed. A handful of people clapped. Some stood there looking stunned. Most were laughing. Hey, she never claimed to be a great singer, and if they wanted to blame someone for her singing, they needed to point their fingers at Sara and Ash for dragging her up there to begin with.

She hurried off the stage and onto the dance floor. Ash and Sara scooted a few feet away. Were they embarrassed to be seen with her? She giggled. Serves them right. They danced with the other women, facing the other way. She began to swing her hips again as another singer belted out "I Will Survive." Probably one of the favorites of all karaoke singers.

"Turn around," a man whispered. The heat of his breath tickled her ear. Macon had finally come to her. *Yes!* He obviously wasn't turned off by her singing.

A tingle raced down her spine, but she acted as though she hadn't heard him and continued dancing. A swirling heat deep in her belly urged her to play a little hard to get. Wasn't that what women did? Well, maybe not this crowd. She bit her lip and slowly turned. She stopped mid-hip roll and gasped. Anger quickly replaced her shock, and darts shot from her eyes. Well, if her eyes could've, they would've. A disgusted snort escaped her.

Ash's voice reached her above the loud music. "What the hell is he doing here?"

Chapter Five

Kylie twisted around at Ash's harsh tone. The high wedged shoes she'd borrowed from Sara sent her toppling forward, and she almost fell right on top of her ex-fiancé, Brett McAllister. What was he doing here? How did he even know where to find her?

"Hey, baby girl," Brett said and grabbed at her waist.

"What the hell, Brett?" Her pulse skyrocketed, and she jerked back.

"Come home, sweetheart. I miss you." He reached out again, but Kylie inched away from him.

She shook her head and swayed. Ash caught her elbow. "No. No. No. You leave. Wasn't I clear enough? I never want to see you again."

"Clear? How could you be clear? We haven't talked since you stood me up at the altar. You could've at least showed up and then called it off. You could've at least answered my calls. It was humiliating enough that I had to call your father's office and beg Billy for your whereabouts."

Damn Billy! People began to stare as though she were the asshole. Her mouth tightened. *How dare he?* She tried to leave, not wanting a scene, but he shifted in front of her. She was stuck unless she outran him. Not likely in these shoes. Screw it. *Stand up for yourself. Don't worry about what other people think.* "Stood you up, Brett? Argh. Leave before I tell everyone you screwed my ex-best-friend, my maid of honor."

Ash and Sara moved forward. "Get the hell out of here, you douche," Ash jabbed his arm with her index finger.

Painful memories burst through Kylie's buzz, killing every ounce of fun she'd had tonight. *Damn him.*

"Go home, Brett," Sara yelled over the music. "She doesn't want you here."

Brett didn't budge. "Not until she talks to me. Not until I know why she left."

Kylie blew out a breath, which sounded more like a raspberry with plenty of juice. Screw it. He deserved a little spittle. "Seriously? You want to know why?" Kylie stepped forward. "What is it with you CEO ass-wipe types? I don't owe you shit." Her finger poked hard at his chest. "I'm done with you and your kind. I'm through with relationships, period."

Her eyes watered, but she blinked the tears back. He would not get a drop out of her. No man would. Ever again. *You aren't being fair to the few good men out there.* She guessed that was just tough.

Jake watched as a guy eased close behind Ashlyn and his stomach tightened. *Who the hell is this asshole?* Jake slid out of his VIP table and made his way in her direction, just in case she needed backup.

"It's over, Brett," Ashlyn said. "Leave and take every other executive dipshit in here with you and get on a one-way flight to hell. I hate all you jerks!"

Jake planted himself in front of the guy, grabbed the dick's arm, and twisted it behind his back. "You heard the lady. Get the fuck out and don't come back."

Jake shoved him toward the exit, where Macon took over, and then walked toward Ashlyn. Her words sunk in and hit solid. Now he realized what her problem was. She hated CEO-types. *Shit.* There went his chance, if ever he had one.

"You okay?" What had this asshole done to her? The hurt and hate clearly shone through her eyes. He wanted to pulverize the idiot just for making her upset.

She nodded. "Y-yes. Thank you. I'm so glad you're not like those stupid stuffed suits. You're helpful and actually care if you hurt somebody, I'm sure." She wobbled on her feet and he steadied her. Her gaze observed his black jacket and black slacks. "Well, you look good in a suit, but um, er, you aren't like them, um, I mean... I need another shot." She glanced at his hand on her bare arm.

"Thanks?" *Shit.* Telling her the truth would end things before they started. Best to leave it where it was and see where the chips fell. She was only here for a few days anyway. What could it hurt?

"Ladies, I'd like to buy this pretty, drunk woman a cup of coffee. We'll be right over there." He nodded to his secluded reserved spot.

Smiles filled the women's faces. "Coffee is a great idea. Have fun, Ky," the woman named Sara said, "Don't hurt her or you'll have to answer to us."

"She's in safe hands. I promise." Then he glanced at the tipsy woman hanging on to his arm. "Ky?" He'd known she'd lied about her name, and it irritated him at first, but it wasn't as if he could throw stones, since he'd done exactly the same.

"Kylie. Ky. I answer to both," she said with less of a slur than a moment ago.

He smiled, and then sat next to her. "Like K.Y."

"Huh?" Her brows lowered, as did her stare. Her cheeks flushed. "Oh."

He laughed when she finally caught on and blushed.

His waitress came by, and Kylie insisted on another shot instead of coffee, but he shook his head. "Bring coffee," he ordered.

"He had some nerve showing up here. You've no idea what he did to me. Two-timin' bastard."

"If he cheated on you then you are better off without him."

Her gaze met his. "I see that now, but when I found out on my way to my wedding, it hurt like someone stabbed me in the heart." She lowered her head. "The bastard cheated on me with my maid of honor, he never cared about me. I should have seen the signs. Brett's love was for money and power. His family had both." She slammed her fist on the table. "He thought I would be a good little housewife. Well, screw him! That is so not me."

No wonder she was getting drunk. "You still love him?"

Ky groaned. "That's none of your business." She glared.

"What is love anyway? 'Tis the question." She rested her forehead on top of the table.

"'Tis the question. I agree. Love is an emotion that hurts a lot of people." Like when his dad ran out or like when his ex-fiancée Julia emptied his bank account and left him. He scrubbed his face and then smiled at Kylie as her head drooped lower. "Hello? Darlin, you awake?" He brushed a strand of her silky hair away from her face.

She lifted her head and grinned. That amazing smile was like a sucker punch to his gut. "No. I realize it now. I didn't love him. I loved the idea of being married. I loved the idea of waking up in a man's arms for the rest of my life. What an idiot I was." She blew a raspberry, like he'd seen her do to her ex a moment ago. "Stupid, huh?"

Damn. The honesty Kylie freely offered him cut through a layer around his protected heart, but at the same time made him feel guilty for not being as honest with her. "Not stupid at all." He'd had similar desires but never indulged in them. "I like you, Ky."

Those long eyelashes of hers batted away at him. "You do?"

While her hand rested next to his on top of the table, he slowly eased his fingers over of hers. Warmth spread through his cold palm. He snuck a glance at her and caught her staring at their connection or had she noticed his watch? "It was a gift." No doubt it would appear odd that security could afford such a lavish Rolex.

Those beautiful suspicious eyes met his. "Know what I'd like?" she asked.

His fingers entangled between her delicate long ones, enjoying the feel of her skin, then he flipped her hand over and circled his thumb over her palm. "No. Tell me."

"I'd like to…wake up with you in the morning." A hint of longing appeared in her gaze. He recognized it because he saw the same sullenness in the mirror every day, but he never wanted to admit it.

Jake was taken back a little by her openness, but the idea had already crossed his mind though it was more of a fantasy. "You really wouldn't. I'm a little grumpy in the morning." He kissed her forehead, knowing she was still buzzing and wouldn't remember much later.

"See. Told you I'm full of stupid ideas. Stupid. Stupid." She raised her cup of coffee and swallowed. "My head is spinning."

No. He would be the stupid one if he took her back to his room and took advantage of this beautiful, brokenhearted, drunken woman. Her head brushed against his arm. What was it about her that appealed to him so much? It wasn't just her beauty on the outside; there was something deep within her that called to him. She woke a part of him that had been asleep for many years. *Don't do it.* "Damn it. Stay here."

He told her friends he was taking her to her room so she could sleep off the buzz. They warned him they would gather all the authors and beat the shit out of him if he hurt their friend, and then they instructed him to tell Kylie they were heading to the club if she needed them.

He agreed, rushed back, and she was gone.

His heart dropped. Where the hell was she? Shit. What if that asshole came back? What if he hurt her? His fist tightened at the thought. If something happened to her he would… Surprised by his thoughts, he realized it wasn't just the situation—it was the woman in the situation. Someone whistled and he saw Macon at the bar with Ky. She waved.

Adorable. "Ky, I'm taking you back to your room."

"I saw her heading this way and followed her just in case," Macon said as he stepped back. Jake caught him eyeing the cute DJ for a quick second and then Macon gave him a sympathetic shrug. "Got yourself a real winner, huh?"

"I'm not normally like this, guys, so stop talking as though I'm incoherent," Kylie pointed at Macon.

"That guy you dragged out of here was her ex-fiancé." Jake said to explain her actions.

"Rebound. So that makes you safe, right?" Macon nodded. "Got it."

"Shut up. You'd have a hard time trusting people too if you were in my shoes," Jake said, then turned to Kylie. "I'll meet you by the door in a second. Stay right there, okay?" He turned back to Macon. "Stop being an asshole."

"Then stop hiding behind your money." Macon punched him on the shoulder. "I'd love to be in your shoes. Wait. I am aren't I? At least where she's concerned." He smiled.

"I'll tell her the truth soon enough." But Macon wouldn't really want to be him. Maybe now, but not back then. No one really knew the hell he'd been through growing up. Sure Macon had seen a few of the bruises in the school's locker room, but Jake had always blown it off, saying he'd fallen. He couldn't admit to anyone what his mother's boyfriend had truly done. And once he did stand up to him, it only got him knocked out cold, and his mother ended up in the hospital with several broken ribs.

Jake left Macon standing there. "Let's get out of here, honey." Ky nodded and leaned against his shoulder.

They reached her floor, and she dug into her small purse. After a few seconds she glanced up at him with wide eyes. "I don't believe it. I lost my key."

Jake thought about her ex stealing it from her purse and then showing up in her room later tonight. No. There was no way he'd let him hurt her again. "Call your friends and tell them you are coming with me until we get your room rekeyed."

Her mouth dropped and then closed. "I can't put you out like that."

Little by little he watched as she sobered up. "I insist."

More suspicion crossed her face. "What is your room number so I can give it to them?"

After she hung up from arguing with her friends who had insisted on ending their night for her, she won the argument. "They like you but they don't trust you," she said as they walked down the corridor.

He slid the access card across the barcode on his personal elevator then pushed his door open. "Here we are."

She gasped, and then lifted a brow as though not believing her eyes. "Looks nothin' like my room. How on earth can a guard afford this?" She paused. "Sorry. That's none of my business."

"I'm not exactly a guard. And yes. Some can." He silently laughed and watched her pluck at the mask feathers around her face. "Some afford lots of things." Macon did. *Bastard.*

She bunched her lips to the left as though she didn't believe a word he'd said. "If you say so." She turned in a complete circle. "Well, I'll tell ya. When I'm done with dis' cat-zena' it's all going to look betta," she mumbled, and then raised her hands in the air, circled around once more and wobbled slightly.

A laugh threatened to burst at the way she imitated a

drunken orangutan.

Her speech sounded slightly better, but she definitely needed to sleep off this buzz before the head pain hit. He helped her into his bedroom and sat her on the edge of the bed. "Now tell me again what's going to look better?"

"Ca-si-no." She took her time with each syllable. "The hotel. I got new colors. New dee-signs. Pretty ones." She glanced down. "I'm so dry here."

He coughed, covering a laugh. What had she just admitted? "Dry? Where?" If it was where he'd thought she'd meant, he certainly could take care of that—once she sobered a little more.

She shoved her palms in his face. "See. Dry."

"Oh." Maybe he was just distracted by her tight red dress clinging to those gorgeous curves. He repeated what he thought she'd said. "I think you said casino, designs, dry skin—is that right?"

"Yep. I'm a designer. I hope to be here, anyways." Her cheeks turned a bit rosy when she smiled with that adorable lop-sided grin. "You have lotion?" Her smile faded.

He arched his left brow. "Yes. But I'm confused. What casino designs?" *Kylie. Kylie.* "Wait. You're not with Edwards Designs are you?"

"How'd you know my last name?" She yanked her mask off. "I need lotion."

Shit. The interior designer. "You're with Edwards Designs? The designer." *Boy am I screwed.*

"Yes. Yes. Yes." She nodded. "It's gonna be beautiful." She dropped back on the comforter with a light thud. "Nice bed."

"I'll be right back." Damn. Of all people, why had it been her he found intriguing and tempting? *There goes my cover.* A part of him was glad. The lie was eating him up. He hurried to his bathroom, grabbed a bottle of lotion, quickly put a K-cup in the coffee machine, and rushed back. Now he had no choice but to tell her who he was—sooner than later. *Not yet though.*

"I bet it won't be as beautiful as you though." That was true. The woman looked like an angelic devil in that red dress, sprawled over his bed. He sat next to her, then poured lotion into his hands. "Here let me. Give me your hands."

She hesitated, licked her lips, and raised her arms. "Will too."

It took a second to remember they were talking about the designs. "Will not."

The lotion warmed as he slid the liquid over her smooth hands, wrists, and then to her arms. Why had she thought they were dry? Her skin felt like the finest silk, and Holy Mother of God, how he enjoyed touching, squeezing the liquid in between her fingers. It made him want to slide his hands over more delicate places. "Nothing can be as beautiful as you, Kylie Edwards."

"I tell you my last name?" She rose on her elbows.

He smiled. "A few minutes ago, remember?" He sat on the bed, ran more lotion along her sexy shoulders, eased down her arms, and stopped at her hands. "Feel moist yet?"

Her mouth formed a cute little *O* as her eyes filled with desire. "Very." She made a goofy attempt at a wink. "And hot too."

What he wouldn't do to kiss those perfect plush lips. "Would you like me to turn the air conditioner on?" His fingers intertwined with hers. Why did that feel so right? Sure she was a bit tipsy. But she was fully aware of him holding her hand, because she focused as his fingers rubbed the center of her palm.

"That's not what I meant." Off guard, she shot off the bed and backed him into his dresser. "I wanna dance. I can't sing, but I'm good at dancing." She frowned. "But then you took me away from the dance floor and made me drink coffee."

Had he made a mistake interfering? He hoped not. It didn't matter. He didn't like seeing that other man near her. Ex or not. He twisted them around so she was backed up against the dresser. "Yes. On that note, I'll be right back."

He came back to the room with a cup in his hand. "Has anyone told you that you act like an orangutan when you're half-drunk?" he asked softly. "You dance like a cute orangutan in heat too." He pinned her with arms on each side of her so she couldn't escape. Not that she acted like she wanted to. His mouth drifted closer to hers, and he placed the coffee behind her on the dresser.

"A what?" she asked right before he brushed her lips. She arched back and frowned. "Did you call me a monkey?"

He reached behind her, turned on his Bose radio and a soft Motown oldie "My Girl" filled the room. "Drink this coffee, then we dance."

She smiled. "You keep feeding me coffee and I won't be able to fall asleep."

"Drink," he ordered.

After she finished, he took the cup and placed it behind him. "May I have this dance, Clyde?"

"Clyde?" It took her a moment, then it registered on her face and she giggled. "Oh. I remember that old movie. My mom loved Clint Eastwood." She grinned, but sadness flashed briefly in her gaze. "And yes. You may, Mr. Eastwood.

As long as you think I look better than Clyde."

Did he dare tell her he was a huge Clint Eastwood buff, too? Nah. Not tonight. "Much, much, much better." He wrapped his arms around her waist, and she burrowed into his chest. God, she felt so good in his arms. She tilted her hips slightly, and he hardened. She might not be able to dance, but she sure knew how to lure a man in. Dancing didn't matter as long as he could hold her like this. "What am I going to do with you?" he asked, breathing hard.

"You could either get me a banana or kiss me." She giggled. Sober or tipsy, this woman was unlike any woman he'd ever met. Being around her did something to him that no one had ever done. He wasn't sure what the feeling was, exactly, but it warmed him throughout.

Then he laughed hard, and after a moment she stared at him. The funny playful girl was gone. How had she completely turned him inside out?

"I love your laugh." Sultry and almost sober eyes and pouty lips beckoned him. He could look directly into her soul through her beautiful eyes, forever. Christ, what was it about this girl? Something he yearned for. Then her lips parted, and he knew in that second he was a goner. *Shit. He wasn't sure how he knew she had him under her little spell, he just did.* For tonight he'd allow her in. Tonight she would be the one. It was insane. Some people say you know when you meet the right person. There is just that instant click. Had he heard that click? "Oh. Hell."

His head dipped, pausing a nanosecond, before crushing his lips against her sensual, burning mouth. His fingers pushed through her hair while her arms went around him, melding herself against him with every curve of her body.

Lord, the woman knew how to kiss a man into delirium.

Reluctantly, he broke the kiss, and she stared up at him with a glossy gaze. "This isn't right." But he wanted it to be.

She touched her lips. "Man, you're good at this. This seduction game. Except for maybe the Clyde part."

What had she meant about Clyde? He couldn't think straight as he tried to process emotions he hadn't felt in a long ass time. "You think I'm seducing you?" More like she was seducing him. "Well, darling I never play. Nor do I see seducing as a game," he said, a little offended. Even if she was the one *for tonight*, he wasn't a man to take advantage. Especially with her.

"If you are worried that I'm buzzed, I'm not anymore." She tried to kiss him again.

"I'm not so sure." He held her arm's length away by her slender waist. No. He was better than this. Even if he wanted her like he hadn't wanted anything in a long time, it wasn't the right time. Soon though. Very soon.

"I'm sure." Her brows bunched. "You don't want me?"

"Hell yeah, I want you. We just can't." He regretted his words immediately.

"'Cause you think I'm still buzzing? I'm not. I promise. How can I convince you I'm not?"

He leaned against the dresser and folded his arms. "I'm listening—"

"I'm not….I just want to feel alive again. I want fun. I want wild and crazy sex. And boy am I horny." Her gaze bore right through him. "But I don't want strings attached. No emotional bullshit stuff." She paused. "And I want you. You said you liked me, didn't you?"

He liked everything she said until the "no emotional

strings attached" part. He'd done that all of his life, but tonight he'd hoped to hold Ky in his arms and let loose the emotions he'd avoided for far too long. Never in his life had he wanted to open up before. That was another reason he knew she was the kind of girl he'd been looking for. Sincere. Kind. Loving.

Sure, it was insanely too soon to feel this way about her, but still, he couldn't help how he felt. There was something unique about her he really liked. And he wasn't sure yet what it was, but he had to find out.

"Sorry. I can't." Were those words really coming from his mouth?

"You can't have wild crazy sex?" She tilted her head. "I've never been wild or crazy before either, and it's been soooooooooo long since I had sex at all. That dickhead made me wait, only 'cause he was screwing Jan, but maybe if we get drunk together. You have some whiskey here? My buzz has gone flat."

Lord did he want her. She had no clue. "It's not that."

She pinned him against the dresser this time and shoved her hand in his back pocket and squeezed his ass. "Get in bed and get nek-kid, Clyde," she ordered.

"I'm Clint—or better known as Philo in the movie, re-member?" Her playful feistiness almost made him change his mind, but tonight he would only hold her until she fell asleep or her friends came for her. Where were her friends, anyway? He side stepped away from the dresser, sat on the bed, leaned against the silver cushioned headboard, leaving all his clothes on.

She jumped on the foot of the bed. "Good boy." On her hands and knees, she crawled to him, sex-swaying hips swung side to side.

Fuck me. He hardened more.

"You get under the covers, and then I'll join you." He eased his shoes off and unbuttoned and removed his jacket, pitching both to the edge of the bed. Might as well get comfortable.

Resting against the headboard, he raised his left arm, and she automatically cuddled next to him as though they'd done this for years. Her head settled over his chest, and an ache filled his heart. Was this the *something* he'd been missing? Just holding someone like this? It was odd, but a nice change, even if she was drunk.

She patted his pecs. "Hard."

Painfully so. "You have no idea." He tried to ignore the way her soft skin made him feel as he rubbed her bare arms. The way her hips melded against his side. The way she wrapped her legs over his lower abs, slightly brushing the tip of his aching cock.

He wanted to pin her down and fuck her until the sun came up and went back down. Instead, they started talking like old friends.

"Do you have any sisters or brothers?" he asked.

"Just me. What about you?"

"I had a younger sister." He ran his hand over her hair. "She was sweet like you."

"Was?" She yawned. "She's not sweet anymore?"

Thinking about Tara made him miss her so much. "Tara died five years ago."

She touched his cheek. "I'm so sorry." She paused. "Were y'all very close?"

"We were." He kissed her hand. "Maybe we should

change the subject."

She nodded. "I was an only child. If it weren't for my friends, I would have had a very lonely childhood."

It was super easy to talk and open up with her. Ten minutes or so passed, he learned more things about her in those few minutes than he had with his ex in over an entire year, he closed his eyes and listened to the soft music. Forcing his desires to calm while he rubbed her arm gently, putting her to sleep. He'd never forget this moment with her.

Her deep breathing made his mind quiet. Another first. He closed his eyes and began to drift too.

Jake woke up not knowing how much time had passed. But it had to be close to five a.m. He brushed his lips across Kylie's forehead, and she stirred. Her gaze widened.

"Hey, sleepyhead. Sorry I woke you. A new key should be ready for you at the front desk. I can have someone bring it up if you like."

"Thanks, but—" She glanced at her dress still on, but the hem sat hiked up to her thighs. "Darn."

"You sound disappointed." Good. That made two of them, and he was still hard as stone.

"I promised myself no more lies." She knelt, facing him. "I apologize for getting drunk. But I am disappointed we didn't…you know. I've been this stick-in-the-mud for so long, and I decided last night it was time for some adventure. Yet, what do I do?" Her shoulders dropped. "Nothing."

"We did dance and kiss." He hated seeing the sadness return to her eyes.

"Still—I had hoped." She frowned and stood. "May I use the restroom real quick?"

What was she about to say? "Right through that door."

He pointed.

After a moment she returned, sat on the edge of bed and he caught a whiff of peppermint. Did the woman carry a toothbrush and toothpaste in her clutch?

"So, how's your head?" he cut her off.

"Completely fine. Why?"

The hell with it. She was sober, and he couldn't resist her any longer. He grabbed her head between his hands and met her half way, pulling her to him. Her eyes widened, and then their lips collided in a heated frenzy. She opened for him, moaned into his mouth, and he almost lost himself. Their bodies molded as close to each other as they could get. Her hips pressing hard against his cock.

He eased his hand inside the top of her dress, pushed beneath her lacy bra, and cupped her gently, then rougher. The harder he caressed, the louder she moaned. He paused. "You sure?"

"Yes."

He tugged her flimsy dress over her head in one swift swoop. In a slow assessment of her lovely body, he touched her waist. Warmth flooded him completely.

Beautiful.

With the other hand, he brushed from her knees up along her slender thighs, over her curvy hips, up her soft stomach, and over her bra. The damn thing had to go, so he unclasped it. Her plentiful breasts bounced sweetly. God he wanted to taste her. Now. He threw her bra to the side and bit back a groan that had been forcing its way out. There was no stopping now. He had to have her.

The panties had to go next.

He hooked his thumbs on each side of her panties,

slowly teasing the material down her hips and legs, noticing they were almost the same color as the smooth skin beneath. "Perfect."

He kissed the nape of her neck, and she tilted her head near his ear, breathing heavily. His tongue slid down her throat, between her collarbones, then he took one pale nipple into his mouth. Every part of him quivered in anticipation.

She tugged his hair hard as he drew it deep into his mouth, savoring and soaking up this moment as long as he could.

She leaned into him, causing him to straighten as she arched her pelvis into his throbbing cock. "So hard."

Hard for you, baby. It had been way too long since he ached in such a way for a woman. Sure, he'd been with many women, but not lately. And it had only been to scratch an itch. He'd been waiting. Hoping. Wanting more. Wanting a woman to want him for who he was, not what he had.

Kylie was more. Kylie was different. But Kylie didn't have a clue who he was.

You are everything she doesn't want. Everything she hates. When the truth comes out, she'll never want to see you again. Giving her one more chance, he paused for a few seconds before he crushed his mouth on hers, unleashing a yearning he'd held back for way too long. Devouring deep inside every delectable inch he could. Though he feared he was crushing her into him, he still ached to absorb her into his body, but a tiny, sweet moan told him she wasn't in pain. Not at all.

Ky moved her hips in a circular slow motion, drawing him in. Closer. Much like she had on the dance floor where she almost sent him to take a cold shower earlier tonight. *Lord save me.* She needed to stop now. He grabbed her legs from under her, pinning her flat against the mattress.

Her eyes widened in surprise, but the corner of her mouth tilted upward.

That little quirk of hers turned his insides soft. "I want you, Ky. Are you ready for me?"

She nodded once, and that was all it took.

He crushed his mouth against hers once more as he ravished her like a starving crazed man. She'd asked for wild crazy sex, and he'd deliver it to her. Now.

He stripped in record time, then lowered his mouth to her breasts, sucking and gently biting. Her nipples stood erect, and her legs wrapped around his waist, pulling his erection against her center.

Her eyes darkened. "I'm enjoying the foreplay, but it's been too long and I'm so damn ready. So can we—"

"As you wish." He cut her off, his gaze never once leaving hers as he slid inside of her wet body. One deep smooth thrust and she took him completely.

Her slick walls were hot and welcoming as she arched her back, allowing him deeper inside. *Lord have mercy.*

Their mouths molded against each other. Their tongues danced wildly while they both sought something neither had in a long time. "I've wanted you since the time I knocked those Cheetos out of your hands."

She dug her nails through his hair, arching higher off the bed, but remained silent other than her subtle panting.

This woman's body was designed perfectly for him. "Wrap your legs around me tight." He couldn't get deep enough. He brushed his lips across her mouth, sliding his down her neck until he found her breasts. He bit playfully, but she moaned loud. "Like that do you?"

"I do."

He held her nipples gently between his teeth, nipping softly as she writhed beneath him.

"Oh, God!"

He took his sweet time, torturing her and himself. Heat bloomed in her eyes as he gripped her ass, pulling her hips up and down to meet his thrusts. At first he worried he might hurt her, but from the heated look on her face, she enjoyed it as much as he did. *No. No. No. Not yet.* He ached to come now, and fought like a mad man not to release himself into her. "Pill?"

Her gaze connected with his as she slowly nodded. "Don't. Stop." She wrapped her arms around his neck. "Bite me again. I'm almost. Almost. There."

Their gazes locked. Something unsaid, an emotion he couldn't quite grasp passed between them, like she knew he ached for more than this physical touch. His pulse increased rapidly, excited yet worried he'd seen something not really there. He didn't want to be her rebound. He wanted more. But for now, this was all they could offer each other.

Slick sheen covered his body and hers, and he caught her bouncing breasts between his lips and sucked with every stroke. The sensual moment was too much to swallow.

I have to open up to her. Tell her the truth. But if you do, you may lose her too.

Her hands gripped his ass, pulling them together. Pulling him from his thoughts. She moaned—no, that was full on groaning—trembling, and finally released a cry of pleasure. Holy hell. He was completely at her mercy in this moment.

"Macon," she said breathlessly.

Fuck.

Chapter Six

Kylie lay in Macon's bed alone. Was she still buzzing a little from last night's shots or flying high because of the marvelous sex? Definitely the sex. Her body had come to life with the mere look in his eyes and the touch of his wonderful hands and oh, that tongue. She buried her head in his pillow and screamed with delight. Never had she had *that* kind of sex with Brett — nor just sex so many times.

They started in bed, moved to the chair. Then on the marble floor and ended up pressed against the glass windows. She glanced at the hand and body smudge prints. *Oh boy. I hope the glass is tinted.* Heat rushed up her neck and landed on her cheeks. Then there was her favorite spot. The Jacuzzi. He'd ordered her to soak her sore body, then he climbed in behind her, and the things he did to her with the hand-held high pressured water sprayer... Lord, she needed to get one of those at home. Heat scorched her face again.

And never in a million years had she known what a

man could do with his tongue. Her nipples rose just thinking about it.

Jan, you can keep plain-vanilla Brett. I'll keep double-hot-fudge with whipped cream and cherries on top Macon. "You can't keep Macon," she whispered, and the words left a hollow spot in her chest.

One night stand, remember? Whatever. At least she hadn't gone through with the marriage. She would have never known what she was missing. And boy had she been missing out. As they say, things happen for a reason. And also, what happens in Vegas stays in Vegas. Marriage? Who needs that shit when you can have this—whatever it was—fling?

She rolled onto her side, barely paying any mind to the shower running in the next room, due to the beautiful sunrise she'd witnessed through the floor-to-ceiling windows. She cast a quick glance at the alarm clock on the nightstand. After six in the morning.

Oh boy. Sara and Ash were probably worried. A pang of guilt filled her. She grabbed the phone, dialed her friend's room, and cringed when voicemail answered. "I'm about to leave Macon's room. I'll see you party animals later."

She hung up, feeling a little better leaving a responsible message so her friends would know she was still alive. Where were they? Why weren't they answering their cell phones? Hopefully they weren't in the casino and clubs looking for her. She'd never hear the end of it.

She smiled at how surprised she was that last night had been so much fun. All except for Brett. Asshole had nerve showing up last night, trying to ruin her fun. Why had he come anyway? Did he honestly think she would still want him after what he had done? Thankfully, Macon had come to her rescue and saved the night—and her. She smiled. It was nice being rescued for a change.

Then she frowned. Did she confide too much in Macon, more than she should have about herself? Talking to him was so easy, and he actually listened to every word as though she mattered. As though everything she'd said mattered. But the sex. The amazing sex. It was a night she'd never forget. Pleased with herself for letting loose for once, she smiled. Macon kept insisting that what they'd shared was just the tip of who he was and what he would like to do with her, but he didn't want to scare her away. The thought of what he wanted to do with her didn't scare her as much as it excited her. She got the feeling he was holding back big time, and a part of her wanted to explore more than the tip—especially after experiencing this much.

Moisture gathered between her legs, but what happened this morning had to be as far as things went.

Macon strolled out of the bathroom with a white towel hanging around his lean hips, and another towel in his hands, drying his dark hair. Her lower stomach clenched. *Sexy.* She leaned forward without realizing, yearning for his touch again.

"Mornin', wild cat." He bent over the bed and kissed her. The clean after-shave scent—or was it soap?— clung in the air, and she took in a deep breath. A pleasurable shiver spiraled through the pit of her stomach. "Hungry?" he asked.

Oh yes. For you. "I did work up an appetite." More like she'd gained one overnight.

"Indeed." He stood back and adjusted his towel. "I'll call room service."

"No thanks. I can't eat right now." However, there

were things to be said. "But can we talk for a second?" She lowered her head and forced her breathing to slow down.

"I'm listening." He swung the other towel over his tan, muscular shoulder, and she couldn't help notice the muscles bunch in his biceps too. He had the body of a young twenty-year-old, but she was certain he had to be at least in his early thirties.

Let me just look at you for a second. Her gaze sought out his chiseled abs and the trace of hair just above the towel. "Yes, I um…I need to apologize for lying to you about my name. I sort of freaked out when you asked me by the pool."

His mouth quirked as though he were about to say something, then he glanced at his bare feet, seemingly hurt. "No need."

"Yes, I need to. I lied. And I hate liars. Despise them." She grabbed his hand and smiled, hopeful.

He remained quiet for a few seconds, then his eyes met hers. "Okay then, let's start with a clean slate." Releasing her hand, he walked to the dresser, then leaned his back against it as he scrubbed his face and sighed. "I need to tell you something, too."

Great. Just when the air was cleared. Her pulse skipped and the blood drained from her face. "You're married?"

"No. Nothing like that." His cell phone rang behind him, and he glanced at the screen. "Damn it. Excuse me a second. I have to take this." He scooped his cell from the nightstand and rushed into the bathroom. "What is it, Macon?"

A wave of coldness flowed through her. Odd. She thought she heard him say, "What is it, Macon?" There couldn't be two Macons, could there? She shook her head. She probably just misunderstood him. He probably said "man," not Macon.

• • •

"What the hell does he want this time?" Jake demanded, one hand gripping the bathroom marble countertop.

"Says he's still looking for someone. Want me to throw his ass out?" Macon asked.

Bad fucking timing. "No. Give me five." Jake hung up and hurried into the bedroom. He hated that he had to leave her. He had to tell her because it was eating him up, and she deserved better.

Kylie was at the door, grabbing her key from his personal concierge. She turned. "I see you called the front desk anyway. Thanks." She sat. "I have to be somewhere."

He sat next to her as she slipped into her heels. Heaviness settled on top of his chest. He had to tell her today. "How about lunch later?"

She stood and straightened her dress. "There's an award luncheon in a bit—"

"Join me instead." He grabbed her hand and pulled her wrist to his lips, kissing it. "I'd like to see you again."

"I don't know." She moved toward the door. Something was bothering her. Her eyes wouldn't meet his, her lips tight.

He followed her, and before she could pull the door open, he pinned her against it, his hands on both sides of her head. He dipped down and kissed her neck. He had to come clean. Today.

"Let me treat you to lunch or maybe more wild sex. Let me show you my real world. Who I really am." Pleading was so not like him, but he couldn't resist her. What the hell was wrong with him?

She turned her head, suspicious, and he took the opportunity to press his lips down the delicate slope of her neck. "You don't play fair, Mr. Eastwood."

So she did remember.

"I'm a man with many names." And she would soon discover his real name. The room closed around him so he focused on her face. Even with black mascara smudged beneath her eyes and her beautiful, thick, long hair puffed out here and there she was still beautiful. He hardly knew her, but something inside of him recognized her soul. Her heart. *Big sap.*

"Twelve-thirty in the lobby by the jester hat fountain." He kissed her lips once more, then stepped back and opened the door.

She narrowed her eyes. "You always get what you want, don't you?"

"No. Not always, but one can hope." It was hard to let go of her, knowing she could find out at any second. He'd never get another chance with her, but he did let go. He watched her disappear into the private elevator just outside of his door. Kylie was different. He knew she was out of her element last night, drinking several shots. And the way her friends drilled him about his info, he almost slipped and told them who he was.

Today everyone would know, including Ky.

She had told a white lie about being Ashlyn, so she'd understand…or so he tried to convince himself. His conscious wasn't buying it, and she probably wouldn't either.

But at least now he knew for sure she didn't have any ulterior motives. She didn't know who he was. This was the first time he'd allowed himself to be with a woman in a while—especially with a woman who had no idea who he was. The last semi-relationship he had, Julia, had been entirely set up. She hadn't really broken down by the airport road. The road he took every weekend to fly his plane. She'd researched everything about him. His likes and dislikes. Everything. *Bitch.* And when he refused to marry her after her fake pregnancy, the real truth came out. *It wasn't even your baby. It was Mark Williams's.* But Ky didn't know the real him. The millionaire. And his money might turn her away. Was that what he was so attracted to? That she'd rather he be someone normal with an average job. Maybe.

But he also enjoyed her free spirit, her goofy dancing, and her needing to be honest with him. A twinge started in his chest, the guilt growing with each breath he took. He had to see her as soon as possible.

· · ·

Kylie stared at her look-what-the-dog-just-dragged-in reflection on the private, stainless steel elevator door. "Oh. My. God." Her cheeks flamed. "Macon kissed this troll? Oh, God." She quickly prayed she'd make it to her room without anyone seeing her. She was a few feet from her door when a woman she thought she recognized—worse off than herself—backed out of a room across from hers, heels and wig in her hand. Kylie hadn't meant to, but she paused. *Lady Gaga?* The woman ducked when she noticed Kylie. Kylie blinked. *I think I just saw Lady Gaga.* No way. Gaga would surely be staying in a penthouse, not on the fourteenth floor. Maybe it was just an author dressed as Gaga? Probably.

Neither said anything, but both lowered their make-up

smeared faces and rats'-nested heads instead. Who was she to judge after the night she'd just had? Her stomach quivered just thinking about all those places they'd had mind-blowing sex.

Another door opened from down the hall. She was pretty sure this was someone she'd seen at the publisher's party. Geesh. Doesn't anyone sleep late anymore? Crap.

She hurried, closed her door, and dropped on her bed. A quick cat nap was in order before her meeting. She woke, then showered and dressed in her best business suit. It was time for her A-game. Knock the management department for a loop. *Kill 'em by design.* She liked that. Maybe she could start on her own firm if her dad didn't give her the senior designer position and kick asshole Billy to the curb. Just wait until she saw that meddling idiot when she got back.

Time for a fresh start. As confident as she was in her skills as a designer, her nerves still bounced around like kernels in a popcorn machine.

Someone knocked. "Come in."

The door opened and Sara stuck her head through. "Woman, we've been looking all over for you."

"I told you where I was because I lost my key and had to wait on a new one, and I really don't have time to talk about it right now." Kylie slipped into her black heels. "My meeting starts soon."

"We knew where you were, but when we tried to come up to get you we weren't able to. You have to have a special card or some kind of code for that floor."

"Oh. Sorry. You should have just called."

"We did. We finally spoke to Macon."

"Really? Well, as much as I'd love to hear this story, I

gotta go." She walked away.

"Meet us by the pool when you're finished."

Ky nodded. "Have my Banana Orgasm ready." She giggled to herself, thinking about when she was the banana-eating orangutan with Macon. She was pretty sure she left a few bite marks. "I might need it after the meeting." Kylie stood, grabbed a ChapStick off of the dresser, and layered it across her still-tingling lips.

Ashlyn pushed her way through the adjoining door and plopped on the already-made bed. "Speaking of orgasms. How many?"

"I don't kiss and tell." She leaned forward and shoved Ash's feet off her bed.

"You never really had much to tell before now," Ash said, and a wicked grin grew on her lips. "But we're hoping this time was different."

Kylie pulled her long hair into a slick ponytail. "Let's just say I never knew what I was missing."

"I knew it. Macon said you passed out and nothing happened."

"He did?" She couldn't believe he'd told her friends nothing had happened, and it surprised her that they had asked. Well, maybe he just volunteered that nothing had—at the time. The thought that he'd protected her reputation warmed her. That man was a true gentleman—though, not in bed. In bed he was a wild tiger.

"We got worried when we couldn't get to your floor. So after you didn't answer your phone, we called Macon to check on you. You were snoring through the phone," Sara said. "Loudly."

Humiliated, her face heated. "Oh, God!" That must've

been after their chat and before she'd woken up from a short nap. Before the best-she'd-ever-had sex. "He never mentioned I snored." He must have gotten a good laugh.

Ash jumped off the bed. "So after you slept your buzz off, then *bam*, huh? How many *bams* was it?"

Geesh. Ash sounded as hard-up as Kylie used to be—and would be again as soon as she left Vegas. It wasn't likely she could find a lover like Macon soon. "Not telling, and 'bam' puts it mildly," she said.

She still couldn't believe she'd had the nerve to go to Macon's room instead of waiting in the lobby for her new key. She paused. She still couldn't believe that the room was his. No way could he afford that.

She'd get to the bottom of it later today. But no matter what, she had the best time of her life. After seeing Brett, it helped push her boring ass over the edge, and unfortunately she'd needed more than alcohol to bury the pain. She smiled. Happily, Macon was just the man to do it. Not at first, but once he agreed, he really agreed.

She had nothing to worry about with Macon. She was having a fun time for the first time without a care in the world. It amazed her that in bed, the blue-collar man had as much power as a CEO. Yet he wasn't greedy at all. He made sure she was more than satisfied before he let her satisfy him. She shook her head. She had to stop thinking about him and sex if she were to nail her meeting. "Crap. I gotta go. Wish me luck."

"Good luck. Knock 'em dead," Sara said.

"We wanna know all about the sex when you meet us later," Ash added. "Spare no details." She winked. "And don't forget we have the grand Masquerade Ball tonight."

"Right. The ball." Kylie grabbed her cell phone and turned it on. Since the ex-jerk had showed up last night she could finally listen to her messages without freaking out at hearing his voice. She really needed to see if she'd missed any important messages from her father. She glanced at the number of voicemail messages. "Forty-eight," she whispered. "Crap. I don't have time." She clicked the phone to silent and threw it back in her purse.

Grabbing the samples and design boards, she rushed out of the room and hit the elevator button for the tenth floor. Butterflies looped in her stomach like they were caught in a tornado.

"You can do this." *Hold your head up and make Daddy proud. No. Make yourself proud.*

Chapter Seven

Jake found Macon waiting near the check-in counter in the hotel lobby. "Where is he?"

Macon shook his head. "Gone."

"Did he say *who* he was looking for this time?" Jake crossed his arms.

"Just like before, looking for someone, but again, didn't say who. He's up to something, Jake. And I'm not certain it's the staff he wants this time." Macon turned to the clerk and gave her orders to print pictures of Mark Williams and to hand them out.

What else could it be? Was he still pissed that his ex-fiancée left him for Jake? That shouldn't be it. Mark knew what the bitch was up to. Jake combed the busy lobby worried that his competitor or his flunkies were talking to his guests and passing out free drink coupons or some such bullshit to lure them to the new casino next door.

Sadly, Mark also still held a grudge from when they

worked together a long time ago. Jake had gotten the promotion that Mark had thought was his. He'd never gotten
over it, and it burned him up, seeing Jake climb to the top.
Jake had only climbed to the top and then bought out the
company because he was a hands-on type of boss. *No, it's
because you like control over everything.*

His cell phone reminder alarm buzzed. *Shit.* He knew
he was forgetting something important when he woke up.
It wasn't like him to be this off. *Kylie.* His nine a.m. meeting
with the design management team. He swallowed. How the
hell was he going to handle this? Shit. He'd have to tell his
staff to cancel the meeting and reschedule with her later.

"Keep an eye out, Macon." Jake stepped into his elevator
and pressed the tenth-floor button. The metal doors closed,
then swung open a few seconds later. His secretary stood a
few feet from the door awaiting his arrival.

"Mr. Royale, can I see you for a minute?" Bonnie pulled
him to the side as soon as he stepped out.

He didn't like her nervous tone. "Can it wait? I need to
see Carol before the design meeting starts."

Bonnie had been with him for seven years, and he
valued her more than she would ever know. She knew his
moves before he did.

Bonnie bit her lip and shook her head. "No. I really need
to talk to you now. Before — "

Jake glanced toward the conference room, the door was
shut. Had they started early? Was Kylie in there? His fists
tightened. "First, I need you to do something for me."

• • •

Kylie spread her color boards, flooring, and wall finish samples across the long wooden conference table. Carol and a man named Tad followed her as she sorted them.

"I'm impressed," Carol said, her hand sliding over the carpet tile sample. "Mr. Royale will love this color scheme." She pointed to the pretty green color chart that she'd named *Forest.* The hues made a relaxing atmosphere, as though one were enjoying a walk in a beautiful park.

"That's my favorite too, but I brought a second option just in case." She started to feel a little less nervous as she pushed the other option on the side of the first.

"He'll go for this bronze chart," Tad said, raising the samples off the table to get a closer look. "Unless—"

"Maybe we could do both," Kylie said. "I like the bronze for the casino and the green for the hotel. Mix both colors within the flooring and draperies, and—"

The door swung open and Kylie straightened herself. This was her moment. She couldn't wait to meet *the* Jake Royale. *Please like my designs.*

A woman who resembled Meryl Streep in "The Devil Wears Prada" movie stepped in the room. *Darn.*

"Mr. Royale had to cancel. An emergency has come up."

Disappointed, Kylie faked her smile anyway. "Oh. Would he like to reschedule? I'll be here until Sunday."

Meryl scrolled through an iPad, searching Mr. Royale's schedule. "He's booked through the week, but I know he wants to meet with you. I'll get back in touch with you later today."

Ky literally felt her posture slouch over. *No. No. Stand tall. A minor setback is all.* "Okay. Thank you."

The woman began to close the door when Kylie peered

down the hall and noticed a man who looked exactly like Macon from the back. She waited for him to turn, but he never did and the door slammed shut. Was the surveillance office up here as well?

"Enjoying your stay?" Carol asked, interrupting her thoughts.

"Very much. Mr. Royale has a magnificent hotel and the staff is great," she said. "I met a few of the employees, one yesterday, maybe you know him. Macon?"

"Of course. He's our Chief of Surveillance. Sort of a sergeant military type personality."

Kylie tilted her head. Not with her. "Really? I didn't get that." Were they talking about the same Macon? Macon did have a slight air about him, though she just figured it came with his position of being in charge of security. He seemed confident in himself. There was nothing wrong with that. There must be two Macons. That explains why she thought she heard him say Macon on the phone.

"Where'd you meet him?" Carol asked.

"Officially, I met him by the pool. Then last night we sort of bumped into each other," she said. *More than once.* She didn't say where. She didn't want to get him into trouble.

"Macon was by the pool? That's odd. He usually observes the casino area only—unless there is a problem."

"Really? How odd." Well, he certainly didn't mind it the other day when he came to apologize to her. Carol glanced at Tad and nodded. There must be two. Ask them.

Kyle gathered her designs and handed them to Carol. She couldn't bring herself to say anything. "Can you take care of these for me?"

"Don't worry. We'll show Mr. Royale your designs and

let you know what we decide before you leave."

"I'd still love the opportunity to present them to him myself if he has a cancellation." She hated leaving the office without meeting him. *Damn.*

"Nice meeting you, Tad." She and Carol walked into the hall.

They stopped near the elevator door. "I think he's going to love your ideas. You'll hear back from one of us real soon."

A door slammed down the hall, followed by yelling. Carol's eyes widened, appearing shocked by the sudden outburst.

"You're leaving at the perfect time," Carol tilted her head toward her and spoke in low tones. "It's highly unusual for Mr. Royale to yell."

Kylie stepped in the elevator, but as the metal door started closing, a woman forged herself between the steel and the doors bounced open. Not smart.

Then she caught the woman sniffling, and saw the tears. Oh.

"Bonnie, wait." A man called out. "Let's discuss this."

She knew that voice. The man ran toward them. *Macon.* Their gazes connected, and he stopped five feet away. The door began to slide close.

Was that guilt written all over his face? What did he have to be guilty for? She glanced at the crying woman next to her. *Damn it. A girlfriend, or worse, a fiancée.* Was that what he had wanted to tell her? Her chest grew heavy, and she covered her burning face. *Not again.*

The metal doors couldn't close fast enough. It was obvious those two had a relationship. She was almost positive, but she had to find out for certain. *No, you don't. You'll be gone Sunday and never see Macon again, so what does it matter?* She uncovered her face. It mattered. "Are you okay, ma'am?" Kylie dug in her purse and pulled out a tissue.

The woman took the tissue and blew her nose. "Not really."

She shouldn't interfere. *Yes. You need to know.* "Did Macon say something to upset you?"

"What? Macon?" The woman glared at her. "Don't tell me Macon knows about it too. Well, of course he does."

Kylie shoulders dropped, and the elevator door eased open. *What the hell was she talking about?* She was more confused now than ever. *It's highly unusual for Mr. Royale to yell,* she recalled Carol saying. So was Kylie upset at Mr. Royale or Macon? None of this made sense.

"Screw Macon." The lady glared at her, then rushed out.

Her jaw dropped, and her palms grew sweaty. What the heck was going on? She stood in the elevator not sure what to do or where to go.

Maybe she'd ruined a perfectly good relationship. Just like her ex-friend had done to her. She punched her floor number a little harder than needed. No. She didn't want to be that woman. *Where's that Banana Orgasm when I need it?*

Kylie hurried to her room, changed into her trusty one-piece, then hurried down to the pool area. After ordering, she sat between Sara and Ashlyn and sucked the frozen drink down as fast she could. Pain shot to her head.

"Ouch. Brain freeze." She slammed the drink down on the small table next to her and caught Ash and Sara's raised eyebrows. "Stop worrying. I'm fine."

"Doesn't sound like it," Sara said, half-hidden beneath her floppy white hat. "What happened?"

"Royale didn't show up for the meeting. He had an emergency." But Macon showed. *The man who charmed Ash's dress off me. The man who'd broken that woman's heart. No.* She couldn't blame him for the amazing sex. She'd pursued him. But still.

"Damn. Did you reschedule?" Ash asked.

"They'll call me if he has time." She waived the waiter down and ordered another Banana Orgasm. Screw this. She would get to the bottom of it when she met Macon for lunch.

For thirty minutes, she pretended to sleep in the lounger so she didn't have to hear any more pep talks from her friends. She felt like a fool already, and she couldn't have them think she was a complete idiot for jumping into bed with a stranger — not that they would, since it was their idea to begin with. Well, maybe not the sex part. It was casual sex, remember? Nothing more. It was good in theory, but she couldn't seem to separate from her actions. Not that she was in love with him, but she liked him. A lot.

A shadow blocked the sun from her body again like it had done yesterday. Her heart dropped. She opened her eyes, expecting to see him.

Disappointment filled her. It was just the waiter with another round for all of them. *Ugh.* Why are you so attached to him already? It makes no sense. Don't let him make another fool out of you. And in that moment, Kylie decided she had to face reality. This was a short weekend in Vegas, and Macon was a fling.

Chapter Eight

Jake grunted behind his desk, shoving files into the corner. "Now we know what that bastard has been up to. Sonofabitch."

"How many more has he gotten?" Macon asked.

"I don't know. Williams offered Bonnie twice what we pay her." Jake bounced a pencil off his desk so high Macon caught it. "Why didn't she come see me? We've been together so long. I need her, Macon."

"When does she start working for that asshole?" Macon placed the pencil on the desk far from Jake's reach.

"Two weeks." He stood and paced his office, overlooking the Vegas strip. "Two lousy weeks. Isn't there a law against stealing someone's employees?" Was the man too lazy to find and train his own employees? Or maybe Mark knew Jake only hired the best.

"Could be. Good news is you have two weeks to do something about it."

"I have no choice but to counter-offer." He kicked the

metal trash can. Luckily, it was empty, but it made one hell of a noise. "I was so pissed when she told me that I just let her walk out of here. I never expected Bonnie to be one of the few that left."

"You realize Bonnie knows stuff. Personal *and* business," Macon said.

He cringed. She knew more personal business than one ought to. She could do lots of damage. "No shit." God, did he know. He glanced at his watch. "Damn it. I have a lunch date with Kylie in two minutes." *If she shows after that scene earlier.* "Keep your eyes open for that scum."

"What? A date?" Macon smiled. "With the girl from last night? Wait. I thought her name was Ashlyn."

"Don't sound so shocked about me having a date. Isn't this what you've been after me to do? And her real name is Kylie."

"Isn't that special? You both lied about who you are."

Jake rushed out of his office, leaving Macon standing there, amused.

• • •

Kylie sat on a bench, fiddling with the strap of her purse in front of the fountain. Her shoulders were drawn down, yet she still took his breath away. Then he lost sight of her due to several people coming in and out of the lobby, blocking his view, but then he'd seen enough. His hands fisted. Anger burst through his pores, and he practically ran toward her.

Don't let him see you sweat. Jake faked a smile and walked up to Kylie just as she and Mark Williams embraced like old lovers. *Sonofabitch. Was Mark trying to pay him back for what happened with Julia?* Flames shot through the top of his head. *You fucking bastard. Kylie's mine. I won't let you steal her too.*

"Get the fuck off my property, Mark. Now." Hell. He'd lost it anyway.

Kylie flinched, her startled gaze widened. "Is something wrong? Do you know each other?"

Jake frowned and faced her. Had this all been a set up? "How do *you* know him? Are you working for him?"

"No. My father's firm designed the interior of all the guest rooms at The Vault." She glanced at Mark. "We wished he would've given us the lobby and casino phase too, but another firm—"

"You designed Mark's hotel?" he roared. *Wait. Calm yourself. She is a designer, idiot.* He cleared his throat. "So you designed The Vault?"

"Well, not me personally. Mark preferred Billy's scheme over mine." She angled her head as though not understanding why he was upset. "But the firm I work for did."

Mark grabbed Kylie's hand. "Come, darling. Let me make it up to you. Since your father called and told me you were here, I've been trying to reach you. Join me for lunch, love?"

"Sorry. I'm already having lunch with Ma—"

"We're late." Jake grabbed tugged Kylie's other her hand and pulled her away before Mark gave his true identity away...unless Bonnie already had in the elevator. No. She couldn't have. Kylie was about to call him Macon. She didn't know yet.

Guilt ate at him, and his stomach churned. Soon. Very soon she would know who he truly was. They just needed to do it in the right place with no interruptions.

He shot a glare over his shoulder and watched Macon and Will haul Mark's ass out behind them.

. . .

Kylie stepped near the valet parking entry and the dry air sucked the moisture right out of her opened mouth. Macon waved and a black Rolls Royce stopped in front of them. "Nice perks for Head of Security." A little too nice.

The driver turned completely around then scratched his head. "Where to, Mr. — "

"Take us to Flame," Macon cut the driver off.

"Who's Flame?"

"You'll see." Macon squeezed her hand, tight.

"Ouch. What's wrong?" She pulled her hand from his and rubbed her fingers. "Why were you so harsh toward Mark? Has he done something to you?"

"I didn't mean to hurt you." He placed his arm around her shoulder, tugging her toward him as if staking his claim. "Sorry, but the guy's a thief. He's stealing Masquerade's employees, and he's worked his way up to our top employees now. Employees who know a lot about how we run this business."

"You sure?" It surely seemed more than that. Could that have been what the drama was about earlier with the woman in the elevator? Had he caught her talking with Mark, or was there something between them. She surely hoped not. "Bonnie too?"

Macon's stare penetrated straight through her. "Why do you ask? What did Bonnie say?"

"Not much, really. I heard you two yelling, and I heard you call her name." She tried leaning back, but he held her

firmly. "Is there something else you'd like to share with me?"
She took a deep breath. *Here it comes.*

"She's leaving me." The words literally deflated him as
he said them. *Ouch. So they were a couple.* She frowned.
Damn it. Could they just turn the car around—now? "Not
because of me I hope?"

He blinked. "What? Why would you think that?"

She slipped her shoe on and off nervously. Men could
be so dense sometimes. "Seriously? The woman got in the
elevator crying. You were yelling. I'm not dumb, Macon. It
looked pretty obvious." She turned her head to stare out the
window. "Take me back, please."

He sat quietly for a second, took her chin with the crook
of his finger and turned her face toward him. "No, love. You
got the wrong idea. There's nothing between us. Not like that."

"You said she's leaving you. What else could you mean?"
Please be something else. She dug her feet into the floor, not
wanting to hear the word girlfriend come out of his mouth.

"She's my secretary. *Was* my secretary."

Like that was going to convince her. "Lots of people
date their secretary."

"I'm not lots of people." His expression was serious.

Relief flooded her. "Oh. Sorry. I thought…never mind."
She released a long, deep breath and kicked her shoes out
of the way. "That's good." But he still hadn't told her what
he wanted to talk to her about. She'd give him until the end
of the night and see if he brought it up again. If he didn't,
then—*then what?* She didn't know.

A tiny smile tugged at the corner of his lips. "My fault. I
should've explained. She's going to work for The Vault. For
Mark."

She took his hand in hers. "She means a lot to you, doesn't she? You can't change her mind?"

Her mind felt so much lighter. Why was she so relieved? She knew. She didn't want someone else with Macon. Not like that. Not now. Not until she left Vegas. Truthfully, if Mr. Royale liked her designs, she could be around more, she could be hands-on, and she would love the chance to get to know him better. *No, you don't. Broken heart, remember.* But the truth was she hadn't thought of her broken heart once since she'd been spending time with Macon, other than the brief run in with Brett. Then the only emotion that emerged was pure anger toward him.

The car stopped, and she glanced out of the window. "Um. What are we—"

His door slammed closed and in the next second he was at her door, opening it for her. *Airplanes? Runway?* "Are we having lunch at the airport?"

"Not today. Do you like to fly?" he asked, pulling her out the car, guiding her toward a small engine plane.

"In that?" She followed him into the cockpit. "So… where's the pilot? The crew?" How on earth had he managed to sneak his boss's limo and now his airplane? Jake must trust Macon fully.

"You're looking at him, Clyde." He leaned into her and kissed her lips. The warmth teased her mouth and left her flushed from head to toe.

"Buckle up, love." He cranked the engine and fiddled with a bunch of dials. After speaking in the mic for a moment, the plane lurched forward. "You're stuck with me now, kiddo. At least for a little while." He smiled that sexy, charming smile—the exact same one he wore most of last night.

Chapter Nine

In a little less than an hour, they landed at a private runway in the backyard of a grand mansion. "Damn. This is beautiful. Whose place is this?"

He didn't answer her, but instead helped her down from the plane, holding her hand tight while they walked toward the gorgeous home.

"You like?"

"Wow. I thought my dad's house was massive. This house makes his look like a mini-mansion." And no one had ever called her parents' home a mini-anything. "Where are we?"

"California."

They stepped into the massive marble entrance. She glanced up, her jaw dropping at the sparkling chandelier. He tugged her into a formal dining room where a long table was set with candles, plates, flowers, and goblets. Sure beats any nice restaurant she'd ever eaten at.

"Friends in high places, huh?" Still not believing they

were in California and in a place this exquisite.

"Something like that." He pulled her chair out, and she sat. She could get use to this.

For hours they chatted like long-lost friends again, and she almost forgot that he still had to tell her the truth of whatever he had to say. She wasn't ready for him to ruin it just yet, though, so she didn't bring it up.

The filet and lobster were divine, but the company was much better. Never had she relaxed and been herself with a man in this way, except for last night. She thought it had been the liquor at first. Maybe now was because she was in a million-dollar executive home being entertained like royalty. Her insides flowed with warmth.

Macon was romantic. Something she'd never truly experienced before. But what did it matter? She had to let him go after the weekend was over. The warmth inside her chilled some. Even if she did get the chance to run this job, it was only temporary. Like her and Macon. A fling. That was all.

They laughed. They kissed. He held her in his arms on the veranda while they ate the best crème brûlée she'd had in her life. This was what being with a normal man felt like, minus the special surroundings. "You never said who the billionaire was that allowed you to entertain and impress girls." She licked the hard-crusted sugar off her lips.

"Are you entertained?" He slid his arm around her waist.

"Very." She smiled.

"And are you impressed?" He faced her completely.

"I don't need expensive things to be impressed. Why are you avoiding my question? Does a secretive movie star live here? Maybe a rock star?" She pointed at him. "Oh, maybe

Channing Tatum?"

He laughed, filling her with a heat she didn't need to get used to.

"You'd like that, wouldn't you?" He pulled her closer to him. "Would you rather be with Magic Mike right now?"

"Well. If I'm going to be honest—no. I'm enjoying the man I'm with very much." Macon's gorgeous eyes and sexy dimples made Tatum look ordinary.

"That's a good thing, because I left word with your friends that we will be very late getting back. They were just slightly upset that you'll be missing the ball though. Are you?"

"No. But when did you do that?" He was mighty confident but not in a bad way. She liked that and liked missing the ball even more.

"Earlier when I went into the kitchen to grab our dessert. I knew after our main course we would be here for the night." His gaze fixed on her.

"You are sure of yourself, aren't you?"

"Not exactly. But I do have something to tell you, and I wanted us to be alone." He closed his eyes for a quick second. "Please hear me out."

She tensed. *Here it comes.* Couldn't he wait until their date was over? She was enjoying this moment too much. "If you think you might upset or hurt me, then don't say anything. Please wait until we get back. Unless you are going to tell me you are married or gay." She paused. "Because that's a long flight back."

"I'm single, and I'm not gay. I think you know that." He stared at her for a moment as though fighting with himself. "Are you sure you want to wait?"

"Yes." This could be her last night with him. Then she

could sever the ties in her mind. First, she wanted one more magical night with the best lover she'd ever had before it was over. Maybe she was selfish for wanting that, but it was exactly what she needed.

"As you wish." He leaned in and kissed her—gently at first, then his kiss turned demanding. Powerful. After several long minutes, he lifted her off her feet. "I haven't stopped thinking about you all day. I want to see you dance again." He nipped her bottom lip. "When I saw your handprints on my window earlier today, all I could think about was being inside you again. I want you so bad."

"Let's skip the dancing." She nipped back at his bottom lip, and he moaned as he carried her up the grand stairs. At the top, he pushed open a pair of white doors. Lights came on instantly. The square footage of this bedroom was three times the size of her bedroom in Phoenix. "Can I move in?" She laughed.

"Anytime, Clyde. Anytime."

"You say that like you own the place, Mr. Eastwood." He said it like he owned *her*, too. She would cherish tonight forever. Her heart felt heavy. There were still good men out there. Too bad she would have to give this one up soon.

Still, she couldn't believe she was here with him. Her one night stand turned into a second night stand. It was nice. Oh hell. More than nice. He fell onto the bed with her beneath him. They laughed, and after a few seconds his smile turned serious.

His gaze lifted to hers. She half expected him to change his mind, but when she looked deeper, past those brilliant green eyes, she saw how much he wanted her. God did she ever feel the same about him. Excitement burst through her blood.

His lips were on hers in an instant. He wasn't harsh, but not too gentle either. Fast turned into a slow drug-inducing, blow-your-mind-into-a-zillion-pieces kiss. Her body and soul melted into a warm pile of mush. Dear heavens.

Abruptly breaking the kiss and sliding his bulging arms under her, he swiftly rolled them over until they were side by side, keeping her pinned against his warm, solid body.

"I want to take my time with you and discover all the sexy things you like, but I was too afraid to let go like that before. Tonight, I'll show you how to really let go—if you'll let me."

Swallowing hard, she asked, "How do you know I haven't ever let go before?" He couldn't possibly know that, could he?

His staring directly through her should have clued her in that he knew better. "Have you?"

Her heart hitched. She thought about lying for a second, just to see if he called her bluff, but she couldn't. "Not exactly."

The sexiest grin, dimples and all, spread across his mouth and she melted. "You will baby. You will." Tenderly, he feathered his lips along her throat while his hand cupped behind her neck. He tugged a fistful of hair in a tight grip. His hold wasn't painful. Instead, erotic sensations from his powerful hold shot straight between her legs, weakening her thigh muscles. Her jaw dropped open in shock.

Macon must have practiced that move to perfection. While her mouth hung open he slid his tongue inside, exploring every inch of her. What the hell just hit her? She never even had a chance to catch her breath before the light-headedness from the lack of oxygen to her brain had her head spinning. Whoa.

He tasted every inch of her, and with tiny gasps, she explored him right back. A sweet vanilla-cinnamon-honey flavor from the crème brûlée earlier filled her mouth, and she clung to him tighter.

Ending the kiss, he slowly brushed his finger along her shoulder. "Tonight it's just you and me. There is no world beyond this moment. What happens right now stays here. Understand?"

Excitement and a little fear spiraled through her. What did he have in mind? Could she just let go and allow whatever happens to happen? *You pretty much already did that the first night. Maybe not.* "We won't ever mention it again?"

"Never," he said, sounding like his word was written in stone. "Do you trust me?"

Did she? He'd been an absolute gentleman before, but tonight she saw something different in him. She'd also seen how much he cared about the people he worked with. What would letting go—really letting go—hurt? A little fun could give her the boost she needed to move her life in the right direction. Did she truly trust him? Her limbs stiffened, but she nodded.

"You give me full control?" He shifted a leg between hers and brushed her sensitive thighs.

Desperately, she wanted to explore with him. Just do it. Her eyes met his, and she bit her bottom lip and slowly released it. Kylie stopped breathing. "I do."

He loosened his hold, and she rolled on her back. His mouth hovered inches over hers. "Relax your mouth, sweetheart. I don't want you to break a tooth."

She giggled, not realizing her jaw had been clenched so

tight her teeth were grinding.

He propped himself up on his forearms, pressed up against her.

Awareness of him took complete control. "I'm a little nervous."

"Don't be. Before we begin, I want you to tell me about yourself. Something you haven't told anyone."

"A secret about me?" She blinked. She had no secrets, did she? "Now?"

"Now." He trailed his fingers down her arm. "What is Kylie hiding from the world?" He pressed a kiss to her wrist, and she sucked in a breath.

"Um. Unfortunately…I…I think I told you pretty much everything in my drunken state last night." She tried hard to calm her heartbeat, but it wasn't happening.

"No. You only told me about your ex-fiancé. I want to know about *you*." He brushed her hair away from her face. "Tell me about your father."

A tightness formed in her throat, and she narrowed her eyes. "Now?" She definitely didn't want her dad on her mind right now. What was Macon up to? Was he giving her an out?

"You said you trust me. Now tell me. Why is it you work for your father?"

She groaned. "You sure know how to kill the mood."

Dipping down he nipped her lip playfully. Heat shot through her mouth and straight to her core. "I'm sure I can revive it at any moment," he said with an arched eyebrow. "You agreed, right? Are you going back on your word?"

Ugh. She sighed. No. She could do this. She could be strong. She fired her best confident stare and jutted her chin up a notch.

"Fine. Why do I work for my dad? Let's see." She thought back to her childhood. Growing up, her father had practically been a stranger. "My father was a work-a-holic, and I hardly got to see him. It was mostly my mom and me. My mom was both mother and father. I tried to get his attention, but no matter what I did, or how hard I tried, I never seemed good enough to get his approval or attention. He loved his work more than me."

She paused, finally noticing Macon rubbing his thumb back and forth over her palm. Surprisingly, the hurtful memories easily surfaced. "So when I went to college thinking if I followed in his footsteps and became a designer like him, then maybe he'd see me differently. Maybe even realize that even though I wasn't born the son he'd hoped for, I still could run the company one day." She bent her legs toward to his.

"And?" He eased his thick arm over her stomach and held her waist tight.

Why was he interested in her father issues? Wait. She hadn't even *realized* she had father issues until just now. Hmm.

"And…a year after my dad finally hired me for a junior assistant position, my mom died. We grew more distant, even though we worked together. He still never saw me as an equal. Long story short, he'll never believe I'm good enough to make partner in his firm, no matter how long I work for him. His own daughter."

She closed her eyes. Damn it. She shouldn't have said all that. But with Macon, it just came out. Like he knew secrets about her that she didn't even know.

He kissed her forehead. "Ky, you don't need your father's or anyone's stamp of approval to be successful in life.

Why not start your own firm or find another one to work at instead of always trying to compete and prove your worth?"

Her lips parted. "You are good. I'll give you that. I hadn't even realized how pathetic I've been until I said it just now." She wrapped her arms around him tight. "I don't know whether to be glad or mad." She laughed. "How much do I owe you for the session, doc?"

"Oh, sweetheart, you are about to find out," he said and then crushed her lips with his.

• • •

Jake knew there was something holding this beautiful woman back, but he had no idea she just wanted her father to be proud of her. She wasn't pathetic at all. She just needed someone to tell her she was worth their time. Something so simple meant so much to her.

And he liked her all the more for it. Her confession also led him to believe this was a part of the reason she disliked men in powerful positions. He understood her a little better now.

His father had never been present in his life, so all he knew was his mother's abusive boyfriends. Most of them drank all day and beat the shit out of him—and/or his mother—at night. It was a routine he'd become adjusted to, but he still trembled when his trailer bedroom door creaked open. To this very day, he had to lock his bedroom door at night. No matter if he slept here in his mansion or at his penthouse at the casino.

He hooked her chin with his finger. "Don't ever say that you are pathetic again. I see a very passionate woman who can do anything she wants. Got it?"

She nodded. "Thank you."

He wanted to see Kylie start her own firm, and he'd help her if she'd take it. She needed to be the one to control her success and her life, not her father.

She leaned into him to deepen their kiss. He loved that about her. What he gave, she returned. He stroked his tongue over her parted lips, then was in her slick and warm mouth again, pushing, seeking—for what, he wasn't sure.

He hardened, and urgency grew in his body. She seemed hungry for him too, pulling at his waist. Nope. Not yet.

He broke the kiss and moved away. "Lie in the middle of the bed," he ordered. "Then slowly remove your heels and all your clothes except your bra and panties."

Her cheeks were flaming, and her eyes were bright with curiosity. "You do the same," she replied.

"Oh, I will. But first I need you to agree with what I'm about to do or we can stop now." He prayed she would open up to him.

She hesitated. "As long as you don't tie me up, I agree."

"Then I'll leave the rope out this time." He moved to the nightstand, watching her as she pulled the dress over her head. Damn. He loved seeing her sweet curves. She lay back on the bed, and he grabbed a sheer black scarf from the drawer, leaving the rope behind, then turned toward her.

Her eyes grew wide. The excitement, easy to see, but he also saw confusion. "No talking allowed."

"Um. But how did you know that was in there? You bring many women here?" Did he hear a hint of jealousy? She bit her cute bottom lip again.

"I said no talking." He placed the scarf over her eyes

and wanted to laugh at how quickly her jaw dropped open. "Don't speak, or I will have to gag your delicious mouth too. But I have plans for those lips, so no speaking, understand?"

It took a few seconds before she nodded.

"That's my girl." He leaned closer. "Since we aren't using rope, I want you to place your hands under your head, lock your fingers together and keep them there. I promise you'll enjoy this. I won't hurt you. Well, maybe a little ache here and there," he whispered. "And to help put your mind at ease about me knowing those items were in there, I placed the scarf in the drawer earlier when you went out on the balcony downstairs. I had a feeling we would end up here tonight, and I wanted it to be memorable for you."

She licked her lips and nodded.

"Ky, I'm going to touch and taste you—everywhere," he said. "I'm going to do things to you that your mind has only dreamed of, but you thought were things too naughty to try. Open your mind to all your senses, and allow me to show you differently."

Her chest rose up and down faster and faster. God he was hungry for her. He moved off of the bed, watching her as he took his time undressing until he was completely naked. She tried to sit up. "I'm still here, baby. Don't worry. I won't leave you blindfolded like that. I promise."

She slowly eased back on the pillow, yet he could still sense the fear below the surface, and it made him realize he had to be a little more subtle tonight. But his goal was to help her let loose and trust him. To trust in herself, too. The first night they were together had been amazing once she'd sobered up, but he felt she'd been holding back. Maybe pretending a little. Not allowing herself to completely enjoy what they'd shared. As though she were hiding her true self from him and from herself. As though she had to put on airs before allowing herself to be at ease. He climbed on the foot of the bed, his hands capturing her feet, and spreading her legs to adjust for him to kneel in between.

He started with her foot, running his fingertips up and down her smooth skin, and between her tiny toes. She laughed and moaned all in one. "Ticklish spot?" He was testing her to see if she would answer.

Silence. Good.

There was nothing sexier than the arch of a woman's foot. It held so many pressure points and was oh-so-sensitive to most. He lifted her delicate ankle and pressed his lips on her instep. She jerked slightly and almost spoke but caught herself before a full word had escaped. She was good.

Ky had the prettiest and smallest feet he'd seen on a woman. He casually slipped his tongue between her toes, and she jerked in response. He had to hold her firmly. The sweetest moan escaped her as he glided his fingers and tongue up her inner calves, her muscles twitching beneath his hold. He eased forward until his thumbs connected, then hooked with the band of her cream colored panties. He wouldn't pull them off just yet, because he wanted to drag out this moment as long as possible. Maybe torture her a little with a hint of what was to come.

"Open your legs for me." She slid them wider. "More." He insisted. She bent her knees and let her legs fall open to rest on the sheets. "Perfect." He angled his mouth, hovering right above her panties. His heated breath blew over her clit through the material. Her hips rose slightly, groaning as though begging for more.

"I want to lick you here," he said. "Do you want me to lick your sweet flesh, baby?" With each word he made sure to breathe hot air over her now-moist panties. He couldn't believe he was actually here with her. He'd never taken anyone to his home before. Ever. This moment meant a lot to him. That she would actually open up to him mentally and sexually. It said a lot about how much she trusted him. Damn it. He hoped she would trust him again after he told her the truth. The lie sat heavy in his heart, and he wished he would have told her before this moment, but she insisted he wait.

She nodded and licked her lips.

"Is your clit tingling yet? Is it hot and ready for me?"

She nodded and reached down, gripping his hair between her fingers.

"I didn't give you permission to touch me yet." He slid her hands back above her head, then bit her neck. She yelped, but he never truly hurt her — only gave her a warning nip. "I'll tell you when."

He eased back, this time pressing his opened mouth over her panties, his tongue swirling, licking, and tasting the wet material between her thighs. He ached to take her fully into his mouth and taste her juices. His gut twisted with a primal need, and he fisted his hands to stop himself from ripping her panties to shreds. *Control yourself. Let her learn to trust her instincts with you.*

She writhed beneath him, hips surging up against his tongue. Her head swung back and forth. Her teeth held tight to her bottom lip. He smiled. "Hmm. You don't like?"

She nodded her head.

"Oh. You do like. You want more? You want me to remove this barrier between my tongue and your wet, swollen folds?"

She nodded again, and a slow smile eased over her mouth.

He tugged barely so she thought he was pulling her panties off, then stopped. "Not yet." She frowned. "I will taste you—all of you—in just a moment." His lips molded over the silky fabric, but after a few seconds his tongue slid to the side of her panties, beneath the material, and between her legs until he circled the slight dust of curls covering her sensitive flesh. Though he wanted to plunge deep into her, he feathered his tongue between her folds with ease and control.

A sharp intake of breath told him he had her exactly where he wanted her. She tightened her legs around his neck, and he had to pry them away and back down. The material was now getting in the way of what he wanted most, but he had to restrain from delving his tongue deep inside of her, sucking and drinking her juices until she screamed for him to stop.

To hell with it. There was no turning back now. *She wouldn't let you stop if you tried.* No matter what happened between them after tonight, he would never forget this moment.

He sat up and yanked her underwear completely off. Her legs instantly bent and opened wide. "I'm going to fuck you with my tongue. Ready?"

She smiled and slowly nodded.

He forced himself to ease down slowly over her moist flesh instead of diving right in. This was probably harder on him than it was her. His dick throbbed like a mother, demanding it be inside of her instead of his tongue. Too damn bad. It had to wait its turn.

Lightly, he flicked out his tongue and barely touched her clit. Her hips bucked up, and he pulled back. He flicked her again. Pulled back. Each time, she arched for him. He couldn't take it anymore. He placed his arms beneath her legs, held up her hips, and filled his mouth with her. Tasting every inch of her. Exploring her deeply. Watching as she tried to wiggle, but he held her firm. Moisture not only formed between her legs—her entire body glistened.

"Oh, God."

He would let those two words slip from her only because she moaned so loud he thought she was about to come, and he had to pull back. Then he sucked her clit again, and she bucked again. He pulled back.

Time to move to the next step. It was easy to see she was past ready, and after teasing her this long he knew the exact spot she liked the most and took her into his mouth, blending a mix of sucking and nipping until she moaned and collapsed her hips into his arms. With the barest of touch to her folds, he twirled his tongue the way he'd just discovered she liked most until her moans proved he could make her come once more without them even joining yet. "You did good, baby. I loved watching your body react to me."

She smiled and lowered her legs. "Next time I want to watch what you are doing."

He inched his hands up her stomach until he reached her see-through, nude-colored bra, then he flipped the clip in the middle and watched her breasts spill out, pushing the bra to her sides. His mouth made contact with her nipple, her body jerked and she moaned.

Capturing her breast in his mouth, he grazed his tongue

around her flesh, and he growled, the low rumble vibrated in his chest. *Take her. Fuck her now.*

She bent her legs, brushing against his hard length. He hadn't planned to allow her to touch him in any form just yet, but holy shit did it feel—"Oh…*fuck,* Kylie…"

He lifted his gaze to her face and caught her smile. No doubt, she was pleased with herself.

She massaged his dick with her knee, easing back and forth. "No." He pushed her leg down. "Not yet."

He moved across her and sucked her other breast into his mouth, this time he took a harder bite, and she cried out. "You like disobeying the rules."

"I'm not a rule-following kind of girl." She bit her bottom lip.

"That's what I was hoping." He angled his hard-on between her thighs and lightly touched her still-slick folds. She eased her legs open without his orders. Damn, he wanted to thrust inside her this second, but then the suspense would be gone. No, not yet. He was almost done. Just one more test. He eased a finger inside of her and stroked until a hiss escaped from between her lips and her head pitched back. "That what you like?"

She nodded.

"How about a little more?"

"Y-yes," she answered with a smile.

"Oh yeah…a little more since you've been a good girl." He slid another finger inside of her, and she arched against his hand. He worked her with his fingers, pulsing in and out, driving her hips up and down until she began to swivel her pelvis in a circle. He stared at her face, and saw the heat building. His wild cat was panting louder than he'd heard her before.

His erection was so massive as it pushed against his hand, wanting to be inside of her more than anything. His own hips were pumping without his control, his shaft inching ever so deeper until his ridge was inside of her. She was so damn wet.

Jake reached up and pushed the blindfold over her head so he could see her eyes when he took her. Her cheeks were rosy, but when their gazes met, he saw exactly what he'd hoped. Lust. She didn't need to tell him with words—her eyes said it all.

She needed him inside of her as much as he needed to be in her. Fuck control. He would take her with all the strength he had. Right. Now. He was already positioned and moved his hips forward. His hand came behind her knees, pushing her legs up and open, then inched inside her further.

"I'm sorry. I can't take you slow like I wanted." His breath exploded out of his lungs. He surged all the way in, his head fell back. "God, you fit me perfectly," he croaked.

She moved her hands along his chest, her fingers lightly pinching his nipples, then feeling his muscles. Their gazes met again, and her hips began to buck against him harder. It was his turn to hiss. He enjoyed each stroke inside of her. "Fuck. Say something. Say anything."

She wrapped her hands around his ass, tugging his hips into her harder, then she cried out. "Stop. I can't. I can't."

Her actions contradicted her words. He grabbed her wrists and pulled them over her head, thrusting faster and faster. As he pounded, she tensed around his cock. Her squeezing him, and lasting for several seconds. Then he released her hands, and his orgasm slammed hard, racing through him, the force weakening not only his knees but his entire body. The after sensations lasted forever. "Did I hurt you, Ky?"

She touched his cheek. "Not like that, but God did I ache—for you. Jesus. I had no clue foreplay could be so…"

He cut her off with a kiss and then brushed her nose with his. "Just wait for the after-play, sweetheart." He smiled. "Ready?"

Chapter Ten

Early the next morning, flying back was rougher in more ways than one. The wind and rain came down hard. Macon continually spoke on the headset. He seemed nervous, but she wasn't sure if it was due to flying through bad weather or what he still hadn't told her.

Whatever it was, she'd rather not be thousands of feet up in the air when she heard it.

By the time they landed and climbed back into the Rolls Royce, she was exhausted from fear. Plus Macon's cell phone rang nonstop, which reminded her to check some of her own messages. Pressing the button for voicemail, she listened to her father asking how things were going. Shit. The next three calls were from Mark Williams and about ten more were from Brett.

She deleted them as soon as his voice sounded. *Jerk*. The last message was from Sara, checking in last night to make sure she was fine. Ky could hear commotion going on in the background.

"I've never seen those that hairy before either, Ash." She thought she heard in the background noise of Sara's voicemail. "There's some crazy shit going down here girl. You're missing the fun—or maybe you aren't." Ash screamed over Sara's voice. "Ky didn't miss anything. She was exactly where she had wanted to be. Getting a piece of ass again. Good girl. Talk to you later." The voicemail stopped.

She loved her friends and was truly grateful they'd dragged her out of her boring life.

The Rolls stopped in front of the casino, and they got out with their cell phones next to their ears. After deleting her last call, she threw her phone in her purse and scanned Macon's face. His quick smile didn't reach his eyes, and he hung up before she had the chance to speak. His arms pulled her into a hug, and then he kissed her like he was saying good-bye. *I'd rather break it off not knowing.*

"Excuse me, sir," the driver said. "Sir? Mr. Royale."

Kylie broke the kiss. *What?*

"Give me a moment," Macon growled from between his teeth at the driver.

The driver stared at Macon. "Yes. Sir."

Macon closed his eyes briefly, then his gaze met hers.

"I'll move the car over here until I hear back from you, Mr. Royale."

Ky's jaw dropped. "Mr. Royale?" Heat burned her from the inside out and her body shook. "*You're* Jake Royale?"

His gaze slowly met hers. "That's what I wanted to tell you last night and the night before. And what I was going to tell you once we made it to my suite."

"You have got to be kidding me. This has all been a lie?"

She bit the inside of her cheek hard. Feel the pain, but do not cry.

"You're wrong. It hasn't *all* been a lie." He stared her in the eyes. "Everything has been real, other than my name."

She couldn't think. Her pulse pounded so loud in her ears. Pain wrapped around her heart. Suffocating her.

"Really? The man you pretended to be is head of security, not the fucking owner of the casino." She covered her mouth. Cursing wasn't something she normally did, but she couldn't control her anger. "So, that's *your* car and *your* house?"

"Yes. Everything, including the plane, is mine."

His driver. His hotel. His casino. Macon—no, make that Jake Royale—was the man she'd never wanted to fall for ever again. "Damn you." It wouldn't have worked out anyway. Just walk away. Let it go.

He shoved a hand through his hair and turned to his driver. "That is all, Alex."

She stepped forward, stopping only inches from him. "You didn't have to lie. You should have told me before we— you know. I thought I was with someone else." *Someone not like a CEO.*

But he didn't act like a CEO. Not with her. Damn. Pain lodged in her throat. "Why would you do that? Why would you let me sleep with you thinking you were an ordinary man?"

"I am ordinary. I just have money." He placed his hands on her cheeks. "There's no excuse for hurting you. I'm sorry, Ky."

"Don't call me that. Only my friends call me Ky." Her body grew numb. She twisted around and rushed into the lobby, leaving Macon—no, Jake—outside.

As she entered, Mark was being escorted from the building once more. "Mark, wait. I'm coming with you."

• • •

As strong as he was, Jake fell apart when Kylie walked away. But when he saw her on Mark's arm, he completely broke in two. How on earth had the sexy designer put her spell on him so damn fast?

Several couples stood there waiting in the taxi line, staring at them. He didn't give a shit. He ran after her. "Kylie. Wait. We need to talk."

She shot him a get-the-hell-away-from-me glare over her shoulder. But the hurt in her eyes was so much worse. The anger. The disappointment.

• • •

Kylie and Mark side-stepped Jake when another man grabbed Jake's arm and held him back. "Where were you last night? You didn't return my calls, Mr. Royale. I need to tell you what happened at the ball last night." The man said to Jake. "Nobody was electrocuted, but some serious shit went down."

"Electrocuted? Fuck. Where's Macon?" Anger roared from Jake. "Kylie," he yelled again. What the hell was he angry about? He was the one who lied to her. *You lied to him too.*

Kylie went next door with Mark without saying a word, but she didn't enter his casino. She sat on the half wall near the entrance for a few minutes. She just needed a moment to think. Then it hit her and she knew it, clear as a bell. She needed to pack her things and leave. Her dream of designing the casino went up in flames, and the small hope of being with an average man was extinguished as well.

"Jake's an idiot. Forget about him and come stay with me."

She shook her head. "What's the deal between you and Jake? Seems like some bitter rivalry going on."

"When someone who is supposed to be your friend steals your dream job from you…" he paused. "I should've become the owner of Masquerade, not Jake."

"But you have this gorgeous new casino. The Masquerade is old and needs lots of updates."

He patted her hand. "When I heard you were coming I knew I was in trouble. I knew Masquerade would look better than The Vault."

She half-smiled. That was a nice compliment coming from him, even though it was direct. "I'm sorry, Mark. Would you mind a rain check? I'm not feeling well."

He kissed her hand. "He broke your heart, didn't he, dove?"

She glanced at him. "No. We just met."

"Time means nothing where love is concerned." He stood and gave her a hug.

"Love? Ha." What did the employee-stealing Romeo know? She certainly didn't love Jake. She couldn't.

Twenty minutes later, Kylie found Sara and Ashlyn in their room. Tears teased her eyes, but she refused to let them fall. Not in front of them. Not again. Before they could grill her, she blurted out, "Macon is Jake Royale."

Their eyes almost popped out of their heads.

"No freaking way," Sara said.

"Why'd he say he was security?" Ash asked.

Kylie thought back to when they'd met. The cashier told her he was Macon. When they officially met, Sara told him they knew who he was. He'd never said he was Macon. But it didn't matter. He allowed her to think he was.

"I'm going to lie down for a little while." She turned to enter her room.

"Wow. You really like him," Sara said from behind her.

"Doesn't matter anymore." She closed the adjoining door. *He lied. He was pretending. I was just a distraction.* The truth stung more than she ever thought it could.

After several minutes of feeling sorry for herself, surprised that her friends had respected her needing time alone, Kylie heard a knock at her door. "Go away."

"Delivery. We can't leave them out here, ma'am."

Kylie dragged herself from bed. "Hold on." She swung the door open. About a dozen hotel employees stood in the hall with massive bouquets of flowers. The hallway smelled like a florist. She wasn't the flower type of girl, but it was hard not to like the dozen or more gorgeous arrangements. A part of her would love to take them all, but she couldn't.

"I can't accept them. Please deliver them to different people on this floor." She shut the door and climbed back into bed. Whether they were from Jake or Brett, she didn't want them. She was done.

Her adjoining door burst open. "Would you look at this? Someone just sent flowers to our room, but we don't know who." Sara held a bouquet of carnations in her arms.

Then it hit hard. Kylie swallowed as she stared at her

mother's favorite flower. Sara handed her a single pink carnation. "For you. I know how much you like them."

"I do." Sara hadn't a clue that more than likely Jake had sent them, but how did Jake know it was her mother's favorite flower? She rolled over, ignoring her friends until they left, and then she did something she'd done too many times this year.

She cried.

Kylie woke with a start when the call to finalize the color schemes with Carol and Tad came. After getting over the shock that they still wanted to use her, she verified that Jake wouldn't be there, but she still hesitated when she stepped out of the elevator, making double sure he wasn't around. The tenth floor was completely empty, from what she could tell.

Since it was a Sunday, she'd been surprised Carol had called in the first place.

"Hello?" A light shone from the conference room where she'd left her designs. "Carol? Tad?" She entered into the room with caution, then noticed someone sitting in the tall leather chair on the far side of the room, facing the window—the chair swung around.

A man built like he belonged in the boxing ring faced her. His hair color and cut was similar to Jake's, but his nose must have been broken once or maybe twice before. "Who are you?"

Wait—she remembered him from the casino. He'd been with Jake outside of the gift shop, and she'd seen him escorting Mark out of the building.

"I'm the *real* Macon." He stood and stepped closer. "Tad and Carol aren't coming. But I had to meet the woman who stole Jake's heart."

"I stole Jake's heart?" She caught herself from rolling her eyes. "Sure." Even if she did, it didn't matter. *He'd lied.* "So were you in on the scheme too? The old switcheroo."

"No, but he told me about you." The real Macon leaned against the conference table and folded his impressive arms. Was he trying to intimidate her? "It was all a misunderstanding. He's never pretended to be anyone other than who he truly is before he met you. He's really one of the good guys."

"Ha. I can tell." Her voice came out sarcastically.

"Look, Jake would be pissed if he knew I was telling you this, but he liked you the moment he saw you and wanted to see if you would like him for *who* he is, not what he has." Macon stood straight and headed toward the door. "He's always been liked for what he has. Understand what I'm saying? Give him another chance. You won't be sorry."

She didn't like that Macon was here instead of Jake, either, but at least what Macon said made her feel somewhat better. However, little did they know, she was done with second chances. Every time she'd given someone the benefit of the doubt, it had backfired on her.

She watched Macon leave before she grabbed her charts from the table, accepting that the design project was over before it began. Much like her and Jake.

He didn't want her to judge him by his financial status, and yet she'd done exactly that, only opposite of how others had.

She judged all CEOs by the few who'd hurt her in the past. *You're an idiot. Judgmental. Unfair.* But why? It couldn't have been all because of Brett. She thought about her life for a moment, realizing it was more to do with her father, with her parents' relationship more so than with hers. She knew this already, but this time it had really sunk in.

The door creaked. "Still hate me?"

She spun on her heel and found Jake leaning against the doorframe. Her entire body stiffened like one of her design boards, but at the same time a warmth spiraled down her stomach and even lower. Damn him. How could he still control her body's reaction to him when she couldn't control it herself? *Ugh.*

She dropped her boards back on the table and threw her hands on her hips. "Hate. I'm not sure if I would call it hate." She shook her head. "Why'd you have to be so successful?"

"I've been poor before, too. Didn't like starving much." He waved his hand in the air. "I don't like being who I am now either, but with you, I'm different."

Her heart banged against her chest. "Different? Seriously?"

"Yes. A part of me had been missing. Now I feel complete," he said. "No longer alone." He hooked his thumb through his belt loop.

She caught a glimpse of nervousness and remorse in his gaze. She realized he'd walked both sides of life, but it still didn't excuse his actions. "You should have told me who you really were."

"I should have and you should have, too. We both started off pretending to be someone else, and I think we both did it for the same reasons. We didn't want to get hurt. Am I right?"

"I suppose." Other than the fake identity, Jake was different from other men in his financial status. She moved toward him to get to the door. "I'll come pick up my boards later."

"Hold on. You see that I never intentionally wanted to hurt you. But when I heard you tell your ex that you wanted nothing to do with men like me, I was disappointed that I would never get a chance to get to know you. I only wanted one moment to be with you, to see if my attraction to you — if what I felt — was real. So I waited to tell you. I was wrong."

A part of her ached to believe he was sincere. More than anything, she wanted to start over. Start from scratch with no lies between them. Could they? Could she let her guard down one more time? If anything, she did feel better that he admitted doing wrong.

"You don't owe me any explanation, Jake. It was fun." She tried to go around him, but he caught her by the elbow.

"We did have fun didn't we?" He pulled her in front of him and lifted her chin. "Was I wrong to believe there was something more between us? Didn't you feel it, too?"

His gaze held hers captive. "I don't know, Jake. Was there?" There was, but she was scared to admit it. Fear gripped her. *Keep your guard up*, she warned herself. *But if you do, you could be missing out on much more.*

"I thought there was." He brushed his lips on her temple. "Can we start over?"

"I didn't come here looking for a relationship." She really liked him, she admitted, or else she wouldn't be hurting this much.

"I get it. You don't want to be hurt again."

"No. I don't, but that's not the entire reason." She thought about the pain she was feeling right now without him.

You lied to him too. Don't be a hypocrite. Give him

another chance. She stepped back, giving herself room to do what she had to do.

"Whatever those reasons are, I think it's worth us exploring. When you look in my eyes, I see something there. Admit it, you like me." He smiled and showed her the biggest dimples she'd ever seen.

"I never said I didn't like you. I do." She lowered her head. *Don't commit to anything. Just take things one day at a time.* "Jake, let's go slow—take our—"

Cutting her off, he kissed her hard and deep. Heat rushed from her head to her toes. What was she saying?

He raised his head and kissed her forehead. Relief showed through his gaze. "Let's go into my office so I can show you how slow and easy I can be." He gave her ass a light swat.

"Jake! You know what I meant, and that wasn't it." The man stared at her like he wanted to eat her alive. And a second later she found herself backing into his modern office as he moved in front of her, stalking her with those devilishly sexy eyes.

"So you don't want me to show you slow, Clyde." He slammed his office door behind him. "You know I've always wanted to use my desk for other things than work." A wicked grin eased across his lips.

"That's definitely not slow." She bumped into the desk. "Fine, Mr. Eastwood. After this one time, we will start slow." As she leaned against his desk, she caught sight of The Vault casino next door through the window and thought about his situation with Mark. "So what are you going to do about Mark?"

"As it turns out, it is illegal to steal employees."

"That's great, Jake. I hope you get all your employees back." A big part of her was happy that her dad had chosen another person to design The Vault instead of her.

"Only if they want to come back. The only person who truly matters to me right now is you." He cleared his desk with one swoop of his arm and lifted her on top. "Ever played Secretary and Boss?"

"No. But I'll be the boss first." Kylie slid off the surface, playfully shoving him against the desk. "Now. Get on up there before I dock your pay, admin."

Jake cocked his head and said in his best Clint Eastwood accent, "I'm not afraid of any man, but when it comes to you—"

Kylie kissed him, shutting him up momentarily. "Don't give up your day job, Jake. Acting is not for you."

"What about stripping?" He began unbuttoning his pants when a pack of orange Tic Tacs fell to the floor.

She picked them up and shook them. "Hmm. I'll let you audition. And if you're good, I'll pay you with these." She popped one into her mouth.

"I want way more than a mint." He grabbed her hips and pulled her against him. His stare shot right into her soul "I want you very, very much, Ky."

Chapter Eleven

Six months later, the new decor was complete, and Kylie was the new senior designer at her father's firm. Her goal had been accomplished, but now it wasn't what she'd desired most. Jake was. She'd fallen head over heels. And he loved her too. *Really* loved her.

"Are you sure about this?" Jake asked.

"Are you?" she asked him as they rode in the back of the Rolls Royce.

The driver pulled up to the drive-thru chapel. Jake looked so handsome in his black tux and a white shirt. God, she could eat him up daily.

"Yes, but are you sure you don't want a grand wedding instead? Every girl dreams of a big wedding." He squeezed her trembling hand. "We still can do it if you want to."

"No. This is perfect. Just the two of us at the drive-thru." She laughed. "Unless *you* want a big wedding."

"Nope. Just you." He paused and wet his lips. "But I

hope you don't mind I invited a few guests and your dad to celebrate with us back at Masquerade. Your pushy friends insisted."

"Really?" Her heart swelled and her eyes filled.

She loved Jake Royale. Not for what he was. Not for what he did. Not for what he owned. But for understanding her completely.

She loved the entire sexy package. Kylie leaned over and kissed him. "Thank you, Jake. You have no idea how happy that makes me."

His eyes brightened. "Good. But before we arrive I have something for you." He reached behind him and pulled out a large banana.

She laughed. "A banana? What's this for?"

"When we dance our first dance as husband and wife you must put this in your mouth, Clyde," he said, and then winked.

"Very funny, Eastwood," she giggled, then hit his arm. "And I thought you wanted me to use it on you later tonight."

His jaw dropped. "Um. That won't be necessary."

He pulled her against him and swept her away into a deep kiss. Tears welled up behind her eyelids at how happy she was with Jake. And with herself.

"I bought a wedding gift for you too." She reached over the front seat and handed him a dozen packs of Tic Tacs. "I didn't know what to get the man who already had everything."

"You're wrong. I had nothing, Kylie. Not until you."

Acknowledgments

Thanks to Liz Pelletier for inviting me to submit this Vegas story and to Kim and Suzanne for being patient editors.

Also, thanks to my writing buddies (you know who you are) for always being there for me.

Lastly, thank you to my family for understanding that writing comes before cooking and cleaning. (Well, for sort of understanding. LOL.)

About the Author

Dawn wouldn't necessarily call herself a bayou girl, (A New Orleans lady sounds better, though it may not be true. LOL) but she does have the occasional gator park itself in her front yard.

Give Dawn anything chocolate and she'll be your friend for life. When she isn't fishing, golfing, writing or reading, you can find her on the beach or watching her favorite television shows such as *Game of Thrones*, *True Blood*, *Supernatural*, *Hell on Wheels*, and pretty much any home renovation show she can find.

www.ingramcontent.com/pod-product-compliance
Lightning Source LLC
Chambersburg PA
CBHW050829180626
46814CB00004B/1525